Dear Reader:

With her debut mystery, *Rhubarb*, author Lou Jane Temple put Kansas City cuisine on the map. Readers everywhere ate it up. *Rhubarb* immediately went into a second printing.

Clearly, her growing legion of fans crave another helping of what Ms. Lou Jane serves up. Who could blame them? Besides the saucy series character restaurateur Heaven Lee—and her parade of ex-husbands—Lou Jane offers up mouthwatering recipes such as artichoke hummus—yum.

Until I read *Revenge of the Barbeque Queens*, I had no idea that a thriving culinary subculture revolving around barbeque existed. A fascinating world, Lou Jane dishes it up with her usual flourish. Well within the mystery tradition, the great combination of murder and food certainly satisfies. What more could a mystery fan ask for? (Well, yes, there's a little sex here too.)

Bon appetit!

Dana Isaacson

Dana Edwin Isaacson
Senior Editor
St. Martin's DEAD LETTER Paperback Mysteries

Also by Lou Jane Temple

DEATH BY RHUBARB

REVENGE
OF THE
BARBEQUE
QUEENS

Lou Jane Temple

St. Martin's Paperbacks

In loving memory of Stephanie Hoffman Jacobson,
a Kansas City original.

REVENGE OF THE BARBEQUE QUEENS

Copyright © 1997 by Lou Jane Temple.

ISBN: 0-312-96074-3

Printed in the United States of America

St. Martin's Paperbacks edition/April 1997

10 9 8 7 6 5 4 3 2 1

I really am a member of a charity cooking team named the Que Queens and I thank my team members for allowing me to use our team name in this book. As do the fictional queens, the real life Que Queens also cook to benefit Harvester's, the Kansas City food bank. I highly recommend getting involved with your local food distribution network. No one should go to bed hungry in America.

Thanks to the Kansas City Barbeque Society. They let me make a pest of myself one whole season. I learned so much. Thanks also to the IBCA, who let me see how they do it, Texas-style.

Linda Price did invaluable work on this story. She helped create order where there was chaos.

Chapter 1

Pigpen Hopkins woke with a hangover. It had been a hard night of celebrating. A county legislator who he had bribed seven months earlier had finally come through with a lucrative plumbing contract to replace all the pipes in the aging Jackson County Courthouse in Kansas City. Pigpen had spent yesterday climbing and crawling around the building, and it was a better deal than he could have dreamed. After figuring out where he could take the inspectors to view the new plumbing, he estimated he would only have to actually replace one-third of the pipes. There was no way anyone could check the rest of his work without tearing the place apart. It would cost a little money to persuade the inspectors to stay where Pigpen put them, but a bribe or two was in the budget.

This had nothing to do with saving the taxpayers of Jackson County money, however. Pigpen planned to bill them for replacing everything.

On most days, the fact that he was going to be able to bilk the public out of thousands of dollars was enough to send Pigpen on a celebratory binge of Jack Daniel's and beer chasers. But there was even more good news.

Pigpen had gotten the call just as he was getting ready to sneak out the back door of his Independence, Missouri, split-level early to meet the other members of his bowling team in the cocktail lounge at the lanes. Pigpen's wife hated it when he left the house at six for the nine o'clock league. She would have liked for Pigpen to help her put the kids down before he went off to meet the boys. That was why Pigpen was in the process of dodging out through the basement when one of his sons yelled, "Dad, telephone." Pigpen couldn't think of anyone he wanted to talk to but he didn't want to be discovered missing quite so soon, so he took the call.

That call was the real reason for celebration, the reason that Pigpen bought three rounds of drinks himself for the entire team. Of course, he didn't let anyone in on the incredible windfall that had come his way. He told them about the courthouse contract and they all laughed about fleecing the chumps downtown. But he didn't mention the phone offer that would mean real money.

Now all he had to do was figure out what to do with his partners. It had been years since they made the promise to each other. And the offer did come to him. Maybe his partners didn't have to know at all.

Chapter 2

Heaven Lee opened her eyes and looked around. There was red hair everywhere. Sal d'Giovanni was looking at her proudly. It was Sal's barber chair Heaven was sitting in and Sal's handiwork that had resulted in all the red hair on the floor. His latest masterpiece was longer than a crew cut but not by much. Because Heaven's hair was wavy it wouldn't conform to a traditional boy's cut. Now it was very short on the sides with a longer wavy red mop on top. Heaven couldn't stand to actually see her hair being cut. She usually closed her eyes and waited for it to be over.

"Sal, you're a genius." Heaven swung out of the chair and started to hug him. The unlit cigar that stuck out of Sal's mouth changed her mind. She headed for the coffee pot instead.

"Of course it looks great. I did it. I just don't know what the heck got into you this morning. What made you want to whack off that long French twist thing?" Sal asked.

Heaven patted her head once more. "It's the Barbeque World Series, Sal. It's coming here to Kansas City next weekend and the first weekend of October."

Sal chuckled. "Don't tell me you and that kitchen crew of yours are gonna try to beat those good old boys from Tennessee and Texas. Why, they'll eat you for lunch."

Heaven started to be defensive and look hurt but she knew Sal was correct in his assessment. "We are adventurous, but, no, you have to have won a major barbeque contest already this season to be asked to the World Series. You have to earn the right to compete. This is the big one, and there's lots of money involved. I am a judge, though, and I'm competing with a group of celebrity chefs for charity. We have a team named the Que Queens. So there.''

"Que Queens. Celebrity chef, eh. Well, la-di-da. Of course you're the celebrity chef of our block, honey."

Sal's barbershop and Cafe Heaven were right across from each other on Thirty-ninth Street. Heaven did have a habit of getting in the news, along with Sal and most of the folks who worked at Cafe Heaven. They all laughed that Kansas City would be pretty dull without Thirty-ninth Street.

"It is a stretch, I guess, to say actual 'celebrity' chefs, but we raise a lot of money for charity. And we have a ball. Everyone on the team is a food professional and two women are really barbeque experts. They've taught us the difference between grilling and slow cooking at least. We won't make total fools of ourselves," Heaven said.

"Don't bet on it," Sal mumbled.

"You'll love this, Sal. Our contest is boys against the girls. We will try to answer that age-old question: Who can make the best barbeque, male or female?"

"You don't want my opinion on that one," Sal said.

"Yes, I do, Sal, but you have to pay to give it. The whole point of the contest is that people will throw in two bucks to vote, and all the proceeds go to the Food Bank. We're going to make sauce, and sell T-shirts and all the extras. It'll raise more money and the whole thing will entertain the crowd while the serious competitors fight it out." Heaven was sitting in a chair in the front window of Sal's, drinking coffee and waving across the street at her friend Mona Kirk. Mona owned a shop called the City Cat. The store was full of cat stuff for the actual cat, bowls and collars, and human stuff for cat fans, earrings and T-shirts. Mona was standing in her front window, as usual, talking on the telephone. She waved back at Heaven.

"I still don't get it, H. What does this barbeque whoop-de-do have to do with you getting your hair cut off?" Sal was sweeping up the red-haired debris as he grilled Heaven.

Heaven was primping at her reflection in the front window. "The smoke gets in your hair and you just can't get it out. We had a practice rib smoking last weekend and everything I wore had to be washed three times. The smoke didn't come out of my hair no matter what I shampooed with. I'm going to be around smoke for the next two weeks so it seemed like a good reason for a new look. You know how I like to change my look every once in a while, whether I need it or not."

"There's one thing you never change, Heaven. You never change that red color." Sal said.

"Not since I found this color and the genius that mixes it up. Renee and I have been together for twenty some years now. A good colorist is as important as a good husband, Sal, maybe even more important."

Sal motioned for his next customer to take the chair, a suit type who had been listening to every word. One of the reasons everyone went to Sal's was for the latest information. "You should know, Heaven. You've had Renee longer than any of your husbands," Sal quipped. Heaven had been married five times so far.

"Now, Sal, don't be mean. Not all of those were my fault. I better go to work. It's almost ten, I've got chopping and dicing to do." Heaven left a twenty-dollar bill in the coffee can where customers were supposed to leave some change for the coffee fund. Sal wouldn't let Heaven pay for her haircuts, so she usually left money in some out-of-the-way place around the barbershop. By the time Sal found it, he just wondered how it got there and stuck it in his pocket.

As Heaven crossed Thirty-ninth Street to her cafe, she couldn't help doing a little dance. Kansas City was beautiful in late September. The city had had plenty of rain early in the month so the trees were turning slowly to gold and orange and a shade very close to that of Heaven's hair.

This is my favorite time of the year, Heaven thought. I love it when nature follows my lead and turns the whole town my colors. The feeling of being queen of the universe, with nature at her command, continued just long enough for her to enter the kitchen of Cafe Heaven.

Owning a restaurant is a very humbling experience.

Chapter 3

Pauline Kramer and Brian Hoffman were having an argument. The arrival of the boss didn't seem to have any effect on them. They continued yelling at each other from opposite sides of the worktable. All of a sudden, Pauline turned to Heaven with a gleam in her eye.

"He was smoking pot out in the alley!" Pauline snapped with much disapproval in her voice.

"You rat, you just wait until the next time you want me to start your bread for you 'cause you're late, you just wait!" Brian sputtered at Pauline.

"Brian, come outside with me, *now,*" Heaven snapped.

As soon as she stepped out in the alley behind the kitchen door, Heaven knew Pauline had not been dreaming or delusional. The evidence was still in the air.

"If I can still smell pot out here, don't you think the neighbors can too, Brian? Or what about the delivery guys who come up this alley every day? What if one of them is an anti-drug zealot and feels a duty to call the cops and report the smell of marijuana behind Cafe Heaven? Have you lost the last working brain cells you had?"

"Heaven, I can tell you're pissed. I . . ."

"Brian, don't try to feed me any bullshit. Everyone who works here knows the rules. Keep your drugs at home. And that's where you're going. Home. Now. Two days off, no pay. Good-bye." Heaven spun around and headed back into the kitchen, slamming the door. Brian followed quickly, like a puppy that had just had its nose rubbed in its own you-know-what.

Brian should have stayed outside a little longer. Heaven wasn't done. "And while you're at home, Brian, you can figure out how to repay Pauline and Robbie and I for all the extra work we're going to have without you. I know one thing you can do is work some of my shifts over the next two weekends at night. I'm involved in the Barbeque World Series and I'll need some backup. Pauline, Robbie? Think of anything offhand?" Heaven knew that Brian would hate being at the mercy of his fellow workers. She knew that he knew they would be cruel.

Pauline was the pastry chef and baker for Cafe Heaven. Robbie Lunstrum was the dishwasher, potato and shrimp peeler and general fix-it man. Together with Brian they constituted the day-kitchen team. Heaven helped too, of course, but she was always getting called to the office or the telephone or to talk to a customer or to hear a waiter's tale of woe. You couldn't really depend on Heaven for eight solid hours of prep work.

Robbie spoke first. He was in his early sixties and had a twinkle in his eye from morning to night. He had survived thirty years of hard drinking and had been sober for eight years now. It was a new life as far as he was concerned. He loved being able to come to work, even if it was to peel potatoes. "Brian, my friend, I know it's a tad against the rules—no one is supposed to go to meetings till they are ready—but I want you to attend a Narcotics Anonymous meeting for my repayment."

"Oh, man, I'm only twenty-two. Let me be a kid, have some fun," Brian whined.

"That's what I said, my friend. The next thing I knew it was thirty years later, my wife and kids were gone and I was breaking into cars to steal cheap radios—anything I could turn into a little cash." Robbie wasn't going to take youth for an excuse.

Brian rolled his eyes. "Sure, man. I'm just a joint away from the gutter. Robbie, don't be so dramatic, I'll go to make you happy, man."

"I'll just have to think about what I want you to do," Pauline said with malice in her voice. "Think and think and . . ."

The smile left Brian's face. "Okay, okay. I get it. I fucked up big time. I'll see you guys in a couple of days. I'm sure you'll have new torture figured out. Heaven, man, I'm really sorry."

"Out, Brian. We have work to do." Heaven was already engrossed in looking at the prep sheet. She stayed engrossed and worked in the kitchen through lunch. Lunch at Cafe Heaven was a prix-fixe affair. There was a choice of a soup or a salad, three or four entrees and a couple of desserts for one set price. The cafe couldn't compete with the good cheap food you could get down the street at the Vietnamese restaurant or the deli, so they went the other way and offered a not terribly expensive, three-course meal—more than a sandwich. There were enough doctors from the medical center and lawyers with offices in midtown Kansas City to give Cafe Heaven at least one turn at lunchtime.

CAFE HEAVEN FALL LUNCH

Gingered Parsnip and Carrot Soup
or
Baby Red Oak Lettuce with Grilled Portobello
Mushrooms and Parmesan Shavings

North African Lamb Tagine with Vidalia
Onion Compote
or
K Triple C (Kansas City Country Club)
Chicken Crepes
or
Salmon with Pinot Sauce

Missouri Jonathan Apple Crisp
or
Prune and Armagnac Ice Cream with Praline Sauce

Gingered Parsnip and Carrot Soup

5 lbs. assorted carrots and parsnips, peeled
chicken stock
heavy cream or half-and-half
2–3 inches fresh ginger, peeled
kosher salt, white pepper, nutmeg, allspice

Cut peeled vegetables into chunks. In a large soup
kettle, cover the roots with either chicken stock or, if
you want to make vegetarian soup, water. Throw in the
ginger, sliced. Simmer until the carrots and parsnips are
tender. Then puree the roots and broth together in the
food processor, along with the ginger. Add enough
cream to achieve a medium-thick consistency and add
seasonings to taste. If you want a stronger ginger taste,
add some powdered ginger. Be sure to season after you
add the cream. If you are using the soup right away,
heat the cream before adding.

North African Lamb Tagine with Vidalia Onion Compote

2–3 lbs. boneless lamb, cut in cubes (leg or
shoulder meat)
1 cup diced yellow onion
4–6 cloves garlic, chopped fine
2–3 inches fresh ginger, peeled and chopped
1 T. each of black pepper, turmeric and crushed
red pepper flakes
2 tsp. each of ground cinnamon and ground coriander

1 tsp. nutmeg
¼ tsp. cayenne
water, olive oil

In your heaviest saute pan, brown the lamb in a little olive oil and set aside. Saute onions in the oil and lamb drippings, adding a little more oil if necessary. When onions are soft and clear, add garlic, ginger and the spices. When this mixture is bubbling, add the lamb and coat with the spices. Cover with water and simmer 1 hour uncovered, adding more water at least once. After an hour, taste for tenderness and continue simmering until fork-tender, which will vary with the cut of meat used. Salt to taste. Serve with basmati or other long-grain rice, or a combination of rice, bulgur, couscous and/or barley. Top with the onion compote (see following recipe).

Onion Compote

6 Vidalia or other sweet onions, such as Walla-
    Walla, Ososweet, or Texas 10/30
½ cup raisins
butter, olive oil, kosher salt, sugar

Peel, split and slice onions. In a tablespoon each of oil and butter, slowly saute onions. When they are soft and translucent, add 1 tsp. kosher salt and sugar and continue simmering until the onions reach a light-brown caramel color. Stir every five minutes or so. This will take 30 minutes to 1 hour, depending on your heat source. Add raisins.

As the afternoon passed, Heaven and the crew fell into an easy silence. Everyone was working quietly at his or her workstation when the night shift burst in to the kitchen on a wave of energy.

They realized they had broken the spell.

"What is this, the public library?" Sara Baxter asked as she put down her knife bag at her workstation. Sara was the grill man at night. She had cooked the world over on tugboats and yachts and was now happily living in Kansas City to be near her grandchildren.

"What time is it? We didn't expect you so soon," Heaven said.

"It's time," Sara said, showing Heaven her watch, which read four-thirty.

Heaven went over to the pass-through window where the waiters soon would be begging for their tables' food. "Sam!" she yelled.

A tall, blond young man came up to the window. He had worked at Cafe Heaven from opening day, first as a busboy, now as a waiter. He was twenty-one and the favorite of all the young women customers and many of the young men as well. The word "dreamboat" was applied often to him.

"How many do we have on the books for tonight, Sam?"

"Only about thirty, H. It's Tuesday, you know."

Tuesday was the slowest night at the restaurant. The cafe had an open mike night on Mondays, where singers and poets and performance artists got to take the stage. Monday was busy, but Tuesdays were quiet. They usually didn't do more than ninety covers on Tuesdays, max.

"Anybody I should know about?" Heaven asked.

"The spice guy from the produce company is coming in for his wife's birthday and so is a friend of yours from Kansas who is now a housemother at Kansas University in Lawrence."

"How did you find out all that Kansas info, Sam?" Heaven asked.

"Oh, she told me on the phone when she made the reservation. And she also told me about the time in junior high when you and the basketball coach . . ." Sam had a gleam of pure mischief in his eyes.

Heaven interrupted quickly. "Never mind, you smart-ass.

I have to go out of the restaurant to make barbeque sauce so send a bottle of champagne to the spice guy. Deutz Brut, I think, will be nice. And for my old school chum, appetizers on the house. I'll write her a note to put on the table and tell her to keep those old stories to herself.''

Heaven turned back to the kitchen. ''Can you live without me tonight? The Que Queens are making sauce at the commissary and I'd like to go.''

''Of course,'' everyone said more or less at once. Heaven scribbled a note to her old friend and set it on the pass-through window.

''She thinks she's indispensable,'' Sara cracked to the rest of the room.

''Only on payday,'' Heaven said as she sailed out the kitchen door. She wanted to check out the front of the house before she left them on their own.

Chapter 4

Bo Morales looked around the barn. His checklist was checked. Everything seemed to be packed. The chuck wagon had been repaired and the horse trailers had been cleaned out for the mules. The flatbed that hauled the chuck wagon would be there early in the morning. The contest meat had arrived from Circle W Ranch an hour ago, packed in coolers with dry ice and frozen blue bags for the trip.

Bo knew he had the option of ordering his meat through the Kansas City Barbeque Guild so he could have it there when he got to town, but he wouldn't think of it. The star Texas barbeque contest winner wasn't going to use some ordinary Yankee meat, no way. Last year in Nashville, when Bo had finished sixth, the World Series committee had provided the meat. Bo supposed it had been perfectly good, but he and everyone else had complained. They would rather pay for their own meat so they could have just what they wanted, rather than have some big poultry company or sausage maker foist their second-rate stuff off on them. This year that's just what they voted to do. The contestants were going to provide their own products. Bo hadn't actually had to pay for his brisket and pork shoulder and lamb and all the rest. The Circle W Ranch was glad to provide him with whatever he wanted. Promoting chuck-wagon cooking was a West Texas thing. The three national figures actually born and raised in West Texas, an actor and two country singers, all wrote checks for anything Bo wanted. After all, didn't the fact that Bo was a handsome, intelligent Hispanic show that West Texas wasn't the backward, racist, poor, white trash place that most Americans thought it was? Bo was glad to be their poster boy. He knew he would make the best of it and turn this into a real career. He had no intention of hauling these fucking mules around the country for the rest of his life. But for now it was fine. It got Bo's picture in the paper. He would let that smile of his get him the next big break.

Bo picked up the cordless phone and left the barn. Now all he had to do was make a few phone calls and make sure things were ready for them in Kansas City. Bo left little to chance. He dialed and smiled as the phone was answered.

"Felicity, may the beauty of your eyes smile on me soon. Yeah, I do go on. I think we need to talk."

Eleazar Martin was tired. He was in his van, driving through heavy traffic. He had been in his van all day, it seemed. The smoker over in West Memphis had been trashed by vandals last night. Aza had had to call a pressure-washing service to clean the spray paint off. They couldn't work it in their schedule until eleven that morning and eleven was when the Rib Shacks all opened for business, so Aza had been transferring cooked meat from his other locations to West Memphis.

Of course this day couldn't be easy. It was his last day in town. Tomorrow he would hitch up the portable smoker and take off for Kansas City. If he weren't so nervous about the World Series, he would be looking forward to getting out of town. His soon-to-be ex-wife was dealing him a fit, saying the child-support agreement wasn't enough, saying the division of the business wasn't fair. Aza had pointed out that two of their three children were already in college. Aza paid all their expenses, so how much money did it take for her and one skinny teenage girl to get along? The lawyer said they had to let an independent auditor estimate the value of the business. This worried Aza for two reasons. If the auditor wasn't a total dummy, he would realize that most of the barbeque income was in cash. He might even assume that Aza was failing to be totally candid about his income not only with his family, but also with the IRS.

Then there was the payout that Aza was going to have to make to his wife sooner or later for her part of the business. He was going to have to lay out some cash; there was no way around it. He wished this divorce thing had never come up. He knew he was never around, but he was spending all the hours working so his kids could have something for their futures. None of them understood. They sure didn't understand how much he needed to win this World Series for the prize money it would bring. Aza felt good about the contest. He was sure he would be in the top ranking when the first weekend was over. But he couldn't just be in the top three. He had to win. So be it. Where there's a will, there's a way. Aza picked up the car phone and went to work on the prize.

"Bo, my man. *¿Como está?* We need to talk."

Felicity June Morgan stared out the window at the water. Charleston, South Carolina, had to be the most beautiful place in the world. She hated to leave it ever. Of course, not everyone knew the Charleston Felicity did. Not everyone was from an old Charleston family with a beautiful house on Bay Street. Not everyone had a huge trust fund so they never had to worry about money. Felicity looked over at the bed where a slim dark figure rested. Not everyone had a beautiful girlfriend to share their bed. She had to leave Charleston this week to go win the World Series of Barbeque. Felicity wanted to go to Kansas City and blast those bubbas with the best damn barbeque they had ever tasted. God knows she had spent enough money on getting it right. No one on the circuit had better equipment or a more qualified team. No one could beat her if everything was equal. But now someone was trying to distract her, piss her off, cost her money. Felicity sat down on the edge of the bed and ruffled the hair of the sleeping figure. Absently she kissed her lover's forehead as she reached across to grab the phone. This problem was irritating her and so it had to be fixed. She dialed and heard a booming voice on the other end.

"Aza, sugar, how's dirty ol' Memphis? Listen, honey, I had a call from Bo earlier and now we need to talk."

Chapter 5

Heaven jumped in her van, which doubled as the restaurant's catering van, and took off. Cafe Heaven was located in midtown Kansas City, an area long on atmosphere and short on wealth. Most of the development in metropolitan Kansas City was taking place to the south and west in Kansas, a situation that had cost the core city in Missouri sorely needed tax money. South and Kansas was where Heaven was heading now.

When she got to Fifty-seventh Street, just off swanky Ward Parkway, she hung a right and pulled into the driveway of a Tudor-style home. Heaven honked the horn and in a minute a tiny blond woman bounded out the door and hopped into the van. Stephanie Simpson was a food stylist for photography and film shoots. She was the Que Queen in charge of making the team booth and food look great. Stephanie's husband was a lawyer, which helped them afford the posh address.

"I'm glad you escaped. I was sure I'd get a phone call saying you couldn't leave your joint," Stephanie said.

"Tuesday is my best shot at getting loose. I can hardly wait to hear all the barbeque gossip. Did Alice and Barbara qualify?" Alice Aron and Barbara Carollo were two members of the Que Queens who were also on official competition barbeque teams. They had their own smokers and campers and everything.

Stephanie was filing her nails as they traveled. She was a fashion plate who received a lot of grief for being the only known barbeque contestant with red, manicured nails. "Alice did and Barbara didn't. Thank God for us. We need one of them for their smoking rig and to boss the rest of us around. We can't let the boys whip our fannies again." The men had beat the women big time the last time they competed.

"Is Barbara pissed?" Heaven asked.

"She pouted all last week when the list of qualifiers was released, but I talked to her this morning and she was over it. She was planning a new dry rub that we're gonna mix up tonight. She thinks we should use it but also sell it to make more money for the Food Bank. Did you bring all the stuff you were in charge of getting?" The members of the team paid for all the sauce supplies themselves so the proceeds of sauce sales could go to the Food Bank. A local radio station sponsored the charity competitions and paid for the meat both teams used.

"Sure did. Honey and orange juice and mustard and wine for us to drink," Heaven replied. "Who's coming tonight?"

"Alice and Barb and you and me and Sally Jo and Meridith. You know, with our schedules it takes twelve to get six." There were actually thirteen members of the Que Queen team but because everyone had to make a living at something else, usually there were only six or seven involved in any one contest. Sally Jo Barton was the food editor of *Snob*, a local magazine. Meridith Goodman owned her own catering business.

"Yes, and having more Queens makes for much better parties," Heaven said as she turned off I-35 and headed west on One Hundred-tenth Street.

The commissary they were heading toward was located in a small industrial park in Lenexa, Kansas. The Kansas City Barbeque Guild rented the space and barbeque entrepreneurs shared it. It was equipped with large freestanding stockpots, a bottling machine, and even empty generic bottles. You called up the guild, booked the space to rent, and brought your own food supplies and labels. It was a cost-effective way to comply with health regulations.

Stephanie looked up from her emery board. "So, tell me your news. How's the cafe? How's Hank? How's Iris?"

"The cafe limps along as usual. We have lots of customers but there still isn't enough money in the bank to pay all the various taxes and payroll and to replace the seventeen chairs that are about to collapse with personal injury lawyers sitting on them." Heaven turned toward Stephanie and smiled coyly. "Hank is great. He's in his surgical residency and when it's over I know we'll be over but . . . until then . . ." Hank was Heaven's boyfriend. "Iris was home for the summer but now she's back in England, going to Oxford and living with her father." Iris was Heaven's daughter.

"And what does Iris think of Hank, pray tell?" Stephanie asked. Hank was only four years older than Iris.

"Iris has known about us from the beginning and she met Hank at Christmas. She says, 'Be happy, Mom.' I know he'll go off soon and marry someone his own age. I want him to have all that, a family, the stuff I've already done," Heaven said halfheartedly. She jerked the steering wheel of the van as they pulled into a parking place in front of a large, nondescript, one-story building.

"My, my, aren't you the generous one," Stephanie said smugly. She looked around as Heaven turned off the engine. "Could it be that we're early?" The parking lot was deserted except for a shiny new pickup with the words PIGPEN PLUMBING painted on the side.

Heaven looked at her watch and nodded. "This may be a first. It's only six-fifteen. We weren't due until six-thirty. Do you think we can get in? I'll unload the van to save valuable gossip time if we can," Heaven said.

Stephanie opened her door and jumped out. "The secretary at the guild said someone else was using it today but they would be done by five. And since they are donating the space because it's for charity, I certainly didn't argue. But now that I see that awful Pigpen Hopkins's truck, I'm sorry I didn't ask who would be here before us. Do you suppose he's mixing up sauce to try to whip our butts again?'' Pigpen was well known in barbeque competitions all over the nation. He also captained the team of men that competed against the Que Queens, the M.C.P., which stood for Male Chauvinist Pigs. Heaven walked up to the door and tried to open it. It was locked, so she banged on it loudly. ''Well, I'm sure Pigpen qualified for the World Series, so we won't have to worry about him lording it over us at our little charity competition at least.''

Stephanie sniffed. ''Oh, he'll find plenty of time to come around and give us grief. He's that kinda fella. His name fits him perfectly. Can you imagine being his wife?''

''Stop, don't take me there,'' Heaven said with her right hand held out, palm up, and her left hand over her eyes. She knocked loudly once more and yelled, ''Oh, Mr. Pigpen, let us come in, let us come in.''

''Not by the greasy hair of my chinny-chin-chin,'' Stephanie sang in a false bass. Pigpen had a beard. ''I think there are delivery docks in the back of these places. Let's take a look.''

Heaven and Stephanie started walking east down the front of the building. The complex housed various kinds of offices and light manufacturing. Next to the commissary was a computer software company and, next to that, an organic potato chip distributor. Every three or four addresses, there was a walkway to the back. Heaven and Stephanie headed around through one of them and soon found themselves at the back door of their destination. There was a loading dock and a garage door, which was closed.

''Pigpen, are you still here?'' Heaven yelled. ''Maybe he went with someone to have a beer and left his truck here.'' She tried the garage door and it went up an inch or so. Slowly, from under the door a thick, red substance appeared and oozed toward Stephanie's high heels.

"Yuck, what in the hell is that, H?" Stephanie reached down and gave the door a big tug. She was strong for her size. The door flew open this time and more red stuff ran out.

Heaven stepped to the side to avoid the red slime. "What an asshole. He must have known that we were coming next and trashed the place. He really is a pig."

The two women jumped over the goo and walked into the big kitchen. It was dark but as their eyes became accustomed to the dimness, Heaven found the light switch and turned on the overheads. A sticky red trail led back to the biggest stockpot and it became very apparent what had caused the overflow. There were the stubby legs of Pigpen Hopkins, dangling out of the pot. His jeans had slipped down from his waist, showing that two inches of his bottom that he was famous for exhibiting, the plumber's crack. The rest of Pigpen was in the stockpot, headfirst in prizewinning barbeque sauce. He looked like he'd been there for a while.

Chapter 6

It was almost ten o'clock at night. The rest of the Que Queens had arrived at about the same time as the ambulance and police cars. It was another hour before the Metro Squad arrived. The Metro Squad was an elite homicide team made up of all the various police departments in the metro Kansas City area. A group of homicide detectives from both Missouri and Kansas worked together for a week and tried to break a case fast. One of the Metro Squad detectives assigned to Pigpen Hopkins was Detective Bonnie Weber, who ten years before had become the first woman detective assigned to homicide in Kansas City, Missouri. She was also Heaven's friend.

Bonnie Weber lit another cigarette and looked around the big kitchen. "What a fuckin' mess," she grumbled under her breath. She and the other two detectives who had arrived on the scene had released the body long ago. The two had gone to tell Mrs. Pigpen and do the paperwork, respectively. The evidence technicians and photographers had just finished up and gone home. The floor of the commissary had a drain and there was a hose, so the evidence boys had hosed the place down before they left.

Bonnie had found a weapon. A meat tenderizer, one of those hammers with pointy metal ridges, was lying on the floor beside the stockpot. When they pulled Pigpen out of the pot it was apparent that the right side of his face had been tenderized, but it didn't look fatal and his skull didn't appear crushed. Bonnie suspected he had been knocked unconscious and then drowned in his own sauce. The particular circumstances of this death would be fodder for police jokes for years. It would become part of Kansas City murder lore.

"Katy, come over here," Bonnie yelled. Heaven's real name was Katherine O'Malley Martin McGuinne Wolff Steinberg Kelley. She had taken Heaven Lee as a stage name during a two-week stint as a stripper twenty-five years ago and the name had stuck. Bonnie was reminding Heaven that she knew her when.

Heaven left the big worktable that her friends were sitting around, drinking St. Francis Old Vine Zinfandel and trading theories about Pigpen. Alice had wanted to make the sauce anyway, but she was overruled by the rest of the crew.

"Hell, we can use the smaller stockpot," Alice said. Alice was a blunt and funny character, short and stocky with gray, curly hair. She had been cooking professionally for thirty years that she admitted to.

"Too gross," everyone else said more or less at the same time. They couldn't leave the scene of the crime, though. Bonnie had talked to them one at a time. At about nine o'clock they had been joined by the president of the Kansas City Barbeque Guild, Paul Taylor. Everyone agreed to call Paul because the guild leased the space and because, according to Alice, he was always good in a crisis.

Heaven plopped down beside Bonnie at the makeshift desk she had created with cases of tomato products. Bonnie was perched on a stool that made her taller than her suspects, who had to sit on a conventional straight-backed chair. Bonnie was a pro. "So, Heaven, just like last time, I save the best interview for last." Bonnie had headed the investigation that spring when someone had been poisoned in Heaven's restaurant.

"Thank God it's not like last time. It isn't in my joint and it isn't someone who dined with one of my ex-husbands," Heaven pointed out.

"But you did find the body and you did have a grudge against this guy. All your little teammates admit that," Bonnie said.

"Not personally," Heaven huffed. "It was purely barbeque. Their team beat our team and he was a jerk about it. He went on the radio saying no woman could ever better a man at smoking meat. But no prize money was involved. What would be the motive for murder?"

Bonnie shook her head. "H, you know better than to ask such a fool question. Life is cheap nowadays. Kids have to kill someone to get a red bandanna. I could make a case that your Que Queens were publicly humiliated and so conspired to get revenge."

Heaven would have none of it. "You'd do much better to talk to the other front-runners in the World Series this weekend. There's $100,000 in prize money on the line, the most ever offered in a barbeque contest. It's doubled since last year. Now that's a motive."

Bonnie rustled a legal pad with names scrawled on it. "Yeah, Paul over there, he gave me the rundown on the folks to beat this weekend. But that's a bit of a stretch, don't ya think, to sneak into town early to knock off the competition? And from what Paul tells me, Pigpen's team will probably compete without him, so whoever did it didn't eliminate diddley."

"Bonnie, can we go? Everyone is tired and freaked out and no one knows anything. As for my alibi, I actually have one. I was at the cafe working all day until I left to pick up Stephanie and come out here. Check with the crew, OK?" Heaven stood up and stretched her arms.

"Go, go, all of you. I guess you know that my partner is gonna love this. You and another murder." Bonnie's partner, Harry Stein, was not a fan of Heaven's.

Heaven looked pleadingly at her friend. "Please, don't let Harry get stuck on me as the prime suspect. There are plenty of people who hated Pigpen Hopkins, Bonnie. He probably has an enemy in every state that holds barbeque contests.

He was arrogant and everyone suspected him of cheating and, the worst of all, he was a really good cooker.''

Cooking was insider's slang for the process that happened at a contest. Trimming, marinating or preparing the meat with dry rub, choosing the woods, tending the fire and the meats, creating a sauce and presenting your entries in an appealing manner. It was all cooking.

Bonnie stood up herself and started packing her legal pads in her big purse. "Get your crew and get outta here. But tell everyone they'll be hearing from me again soon. And Heaven . . ."

Heaven stopped her retreat and looked back at Bonnie.

"Love your new haircut. Don't leave town," Bonnie said with a smile.

Chapter 7

It was Thursday afternoon and the Que Queens were trying again. This time they had convened in the Cafe Heaven kitchen to make up the dry rub. Part of the group would go out to the scene of the crime and mix and bottle the sauce. They had come to the cafe because Heaven was doing Brian's work and couldn't leave.

Que Queens' Royal Rub

¼ cup mixed peppercorns: black, white and pink
¼ cup mustard seeds
¼ cup sesame seeds, lightly toasted
¼ cup New Mexican ground red chili
¼ cup brown sugar
¼ cup kosher salt
¼ cup hot Hungarian paprika
1 dried ancho chili
1 T. each: cinnamon, cumin, rubbed sage, cayenne, allspice, dried thyme and dried tarragon

Combine the peppercorns, mustard seeds, sesame seeds, salt and the ancho chili in the food processor and pulverize. Combine this mixture with all the other ingredients, taking care to mix carefully as it will cause sneezing. Spread on baking sheets and toast in the oven lightly, about 10 minutes at 325 degrees. The toasting brings out the natural oils in the spices and develops the flavor more fully. Store in an airtight container in the freezer.

Barbara Carollo, a chef at an Italian restaurant near the River Market, was taking a few hours off between lunch and dinner. Barbara was from a big southern Italian family herself and had the beautiful dark eyes and hair to prove it. She had been born to the stove and started working in her uncle's cafe when she was twelve. Now, at twenty-three, she had stepped up to the plate in her own kitchen and was winning rave reviews.

Sally Jo Barton was one of the people who had given Barbara a rave review. In her capacity as food editor for *Snob*, Kansas City's society magazine, and as food editor for a business magazine, Sally Jo could make or break a career. A pretty, thirtysomething, Kansas City blue blood, Sally Jo loved her involvement with these food professionals. It was her walk on the wild side and it drove her country-club husband crazy.

Meridith Goodman had no husband to drive crazy, but it wasn't because she hadn't been asked. Like Heaven, Meridith was a stunning redhead. Unlike Heaven, her hair color was natural. Meridith had a plan for her life and career and it didn't include a partner right now. She had talked her parents into letting her attend the Culinary Institute of America instead of Smith like her mother and grandmother had. After graduation, she had made a business plan and talked her parents into loaning her the money to start her own catering business. That had been five years ago and she had just finished paying off that loan. Meridith was totally serious about food and her profession. Much too serious, as far as Heaven was concerned. Thank goodness Stephanie was there to provide some levity.

The kitchen was noisy and crowded. Robbie and Pauline tried to stay out of the way. Barbara and Meridith each had big stainless steel bowls and were gently stirring seeds, chilis, spices and kosher salt together. The other two Queens were measuring out the spices and throwing them in the bowls according to Barbara's recipe. Heaven was prepping food for dinner at Cafe Heaven.

Barbara looked up to see Stephanie opening the cayenne container. "Be careful. Don't breathe," she said.

"Thanks a lot," Stephanie replied.

"No, I mean don't inhale right over the cayenne. It will steal your breath away or make you sneeze. Turn your head to the side to breathe," Barbara explained.

Heaven wanted the latest scoop. "So what's the news? What about Mrs. Pigpen? Did she confess she snuck in and beaned her dearly beloved with the meat cleaver?"

Sally Jo shook her head, her smooth brown pageboy flying. "Amazingly enough, the word is she is truly sad about the death of her spouse. They have two kids in junior high school and Pigpen was a busy plumber. I'm sure the loss of income would be enough to upset you, even if the income was provided by a slob like him. The funeral is tomorrow morning when some of the World Series contestants will already be in town." The qualifying teams had to be checked in at the contest site by six Friday evening.

Stephanie waved the cayenne container at Sally Jo like she had been a naughty schoolgirl. "You're a bitch. Just because the deceased happened to say your chicken was more like beef jerky than poultry at our last contest, you should be more generous with the departed."

Sally Jo was unfazed. "Remember, the bastard said our on-site setup looked like a Chinese whorehouse. You weren't too fond of Mr. Hopkins yourself after that crack."

The back door of the kitchen swung open and Detective Harry Stein ambled in. The usual sneer that passed for a smile on Harry's face was in place. "So, he insulted your chicken and your day-cor, did he? And then you 'Queens' just happened to be the ones that found him facedown in the ketchup. Why, that seems just too convenient for me."

Heaven jumped in like a mother hen defending her chicks. "Well, Detective, have you taken to eavesdropping outside doors?"

"Whatever it takes, Heaven. Whatever it takes," Harry responded.

"Ladies, this is Detective Bonnie Weber's partner, Harry Stein. Watch your back," Heaven said with a snarl. "I didn't know you were on the Metro Squad, Harry. I thought it was only for the best ace detectives."

At this moment, Pauline and Robbie, who had met Detective Stein the previous spring, jumped in. They saw trouble ahead and tried to head it off with food. "Would you like a cup of coffee?" Robbie offered in his most pleasant voice. "A piece of green apple pie, perhaps? It's the season for green apples," Pauline added.

Harry Stein's eyes had turned to slits after the Metro Squad comment. "Can it," he growled in the direction of Robbie. He walked over to the bowls filled with the dry-rub ingredients and sniffed. Barbara Carollo opened her mouth to offer a helpful warning about the spices but closed it again quickly. "What's this?" he asked no one in particular.

Sally Jo Barton took the challenge. "Why, Detective, it's a dry rub to put on your meat," Sally said in her best private-school voice. "Oh, my, I didn't mean *your* meat. I meant meat in general, I meant our meat, I, I . . ." Sally looked around for help and then down at Harry Stein's groin area. She just couldn't help herself.

The detective was actually blushing. "Yeah, yeah, I get the idea. I think I'd better just take a little sample down to the lab, just to make sure what the hell this bunch is cookin' up." He whipped an evidence bag out of his inside coat pocket and looked around for a spoon. "Just for your information, Heaven, I'm not on the Metro Squad this year but I figure my partner's problems are my problems. And you're a problem again. And a suspect, as far as I'm concerned." Harry decided to be macho and stuck his hand in the spice mix. He lifted out about a tablespoon in his hand but more than a tablespoon of dry rub was stirred up by the intrusion. A haze of spices circled his head. Soon Harry's nose was wiggling. He sneezed at least twelve times in rapid succession. The cayenne and chilis and paprika and cracked black, white and pink peppercorns had done their work. Everyone in the kitchen was working hard at suppressing laughter. Everyone but Harry Stein, of course.

"Very funny, Heaven, very funny. You just wait. Remember, he who laughs last," Harry had zipped up his bag of dry rub and was heading for the door, rubbing his nose with his handkerchief. He paused for maximum drama. "By the way, ladies, I got all your names and addresses from the Barbeque Guild. I checked you all out and you'll be glad to know there's only one of you with a police record. That's the famous felon, Katy O'Malley, aka Heaven Lee. Heaven, I'm right behind you." With that twist of the knife, Harry Stein disappeared out the kitchen door.

Everyone looked at Heaven. She opened her mouth but before she could say anything, Stephanie jumped in. "You weren't all in town in 1983, but Heaven used to be a lawyer, after she was married to an English rock star and a famous painter dumped her and she arranged a major drug deal, you know, not for herself but, anyway, she didn't have to go to jail but she couldn't be a lawyer anymore." Stephanie stopped before she shut down from lack of oxygen.

Sally Jo, not to be outdone, said, "I knew that."

"Meridith, you haven't moved since the creep descended. Are you all right?" Heaven asked. She didn't try to hide her sordid past but it wasn't the kind of thing that came up too often with new friends.

Meridith took Barbara's bowl of dry rub and dumped it slowly in the trash can, slowly so it wouldn't do to the rest of them what it had done to Harry Stein. "There is just no excuse for his bad behavior. I'm sorry everyone, but I will not put dry rub that has that man's germs spread over it on my ribs. Of course, it's almost worth the irritation of having to do something twice to have seen the look on his face when he was on the ninth sneeze. Pure panic. I think he thought he was goin' to die.''

At that reminder of Harry Stein's discomfort, the whole kitchen burst into laughter.

Chapter 8

Simone Springer was grumpy. She still had jet lag, thanks to her trip from Paris. Her first day in New York had been spent with her publisher, her agent and her lawyers, who were working on the contract for her next cookbook. Tomorrow she had to cook at the James Beard House. Her assistant was prepping for the Beard House dinner even as she rode in her seventh taxi of the day. The day after tomorrow she had to fly to Kansas City, of all places, to judge the World Series of Barbeque. She had been furious with her agent for agreeing to the gig until she heard who else would be there. Now she couldn't wait. It was about time to tie up those particular loose ends. She would finally finish some very old business, but it would take some planning. She didn't have much time, that was certain. Simone shoved a copy of *Restaurant News* in her bag, the one telling about the launch of a new celebrity fast-food chain.

"Taxi, right here is fine." Simone pushed money at the cabbie and jumped out, heading directly to the pay phone on the corner.

Simone smiled at the phone as though it were a photographer. "Hello, I'm going to be a judge at your barbeque contest and I just need a little more information. Would you mind telling me who's in charge?"

*　　*　　*

Dwight Brooks was having a great year. His album, *Tennessee Stud,* had gone platinum. He had won the Country Music Association Performer of the Year award. Now he was going to beat Kenny Rogers in the fast-food game. The contracts had been signed on Monday. The real estate lawyer had the first twenty locations pinpointed and the start-up costs estimated. Now all he needed was someone who knew about goddamn barbeque. Of course, he had told everyone he was an expert on the subject, told his partners the barbeque was the least of their worries. He needed his luck to hold until he found help to put this deal on the road.

He was sure he would find what he was looking for in Kansas City. That's why he had wanted to judge the World Series of Barbeque. It couldn't have come at a better time for ol' Dwight, yes sir. Now if he could just get what he needed without paying for it, it would be even more fun. Just like he did with those two songs that he borrowed from that sweet little blonde's desk in Nashville last year. One of those songs had been a number one single for him. The little lady hadn't said a word, not wanting her husband to hear the gory details of how Dwight got his hands on them. He sure would like another chance like that to fall in his lap. But you couldn't always wait for chance. Sometimes you had to make things happen. That was one of Dwight's specialties and he chuckled as he picked up the phone. This was already fun.

Dwight cleared his throat while he waited for the phone to be answered. His voice was his instrument, after all.

''Hello, sugar. Let me speak to the boss man. Have I got a deal for him.''

Chapter 9

Heaven looked up at the kitchen clock. It was eight-thirty at night on Thursday and the wheel was clear. That meant that Sara and Heaven and the rest of the crew had fed everyone who was currently in the restaurant and all the tickets were back in the hands of the waiters.

"I'm going to see what's left on the books, and if it's almost over, I'm going to go out to the commissary and bottle this dry rub. The rest of the team should be done with the sauce bottling about the time I get there," Heaven said.

Heaven went through the kitchen doors to the cool dimness of the dining room. The tables were almost all full, there was a great Ella Fitzgerald CD playing over the speakers and the sound of laughter was in the air. For one minute, Heaven looked around and remembered why she had wanted a restaurant in the first place. She walked to the front of the bar where Murray Steinblatz held forth. Murray was the host on Mondays, Fridays, and Saturdays. Heaven had asked him to work a few extra days, like tonight, so she could be involved in this barbeque deal. Murray was involved too, as a celebrity judge, but he only had to show up on Saturday afternoon.

Murray Steinblatz wasn't a celebrity in Kansas City for food, although he now worked in a restaurant. Murray was a native son who went off to journalism school at Columbia, and then a major metropolitan newspaper, the *New York*

Times. He won two Pulitzer Prizes. Then his wife was killed in New York street violence and Murray gave up and came back home to Kansas City. He didn't do much for a year or so except walk around Loose Park in a haze of pain and self-pity. When Cafe Heaven opened, Murray asked Heaven for a job. He knew that if he didn't start being around people again he would be lost in his grief forever. So Murray worked the room at Cafe Heaven, using the same powers of observation that had made him such a good reporter to make sure everyone was entertained and comfortable. Heaven and the kitchen took care of the well-fed part.

"Murray, what's left?" Heaven asked.

"Not much, babe. There are two four-tops due at nine and the maestro is bringing in the visiting artist, an oboe player, after rehearsals at ten." Because Cafe Heaven was open late, even during the week, the symphony and other artistic groups knew they could entertain and eat after ten.

"Then I'm going to split and bottle my dry rub," Heaven said as she looked around the room.

"Sounds like a personal problem to me," Joe Long wise-cracked. He and Chris Snyder were waiters at Cafe Heaven and also the producers of the Monday night open-mike shows. They both headed toward Heaven. "Heaven, I don't really know about the World Series of Barbeque." This came from a morose figure sitting at the bar. It was Jumpin' Jack, who was completely clad in Desert Storm camouflage. Jack just recently had switched over from the Vietnam-era camo he had been wearing for years. His clothes had no relation to a former career in the military, however. Jack was the son of a rich couple who lived in fashionable Mission Hills and paid Jack's bills so he would stay away. Jack's largest monthly expense was his therapist, who tried to keep Jack out of mental health institutions. Jack's jungle was the neighborhood around Cafe Heaven. He knew the Thirty-ninth Street area like the back of his hand and his one-man surveillance of the neighborhood had saved Heaven's life a few months ago. Jack always had a bar stool at Cafe Heaven as far as Heaven was concerned.

"That was going to be our question exactly. What is the World Series of Barbeque?" Chris asked.

"Well, last year was the first year for it, guys. Barbeque contests have grown so much in the last ten years that the different societies and organizations across the country decided it was time for some kind of a grand finale to the contest season," Heaven explained.

"Next question. What is this party we're having here on Sunday night for judges? Is this some bar association thing?" Joe added.

"Different kind of judging, Joe. The party here on Sunday is for the barbeque contest judges and some of the teams. The Guild didn't want to have it in one barbeque restaurant and piss the other barbeque restaurants off, so they asked me. Neutral ground, so to speak," Heaven explained.

Jumpin' Jack asked for more details. "Will this World Series be like baseball, one team from each city?"

Heaven shook her head. "The top fifty teams from around the country will compete in a different major barbeque city each year. The teams got chosen by winning a state championship or winning a contest that had more than fifty teams in it. There were more than fifty of those winners so they took the total points the team had scored during the season. You know, someone might win with perfect ten scores and someone else might win with eights. They have this computerized system of keeping track. So, the teams who won the state or other big contests are the potential team pool, and out of them, the teams with the most points scored are the teams invited to the World Series." Heaven looked around her. A small crowd had formed. Sam had joined Murray, Chris, Joe, and Jumpin' Jack in this barbeque contest workshop. "Is anybody paying attention to the floor?" she asked.

"It's cool," Sam said. "The busboy is pouring coffee,

I'm watching the window for desserts. Boss, how do ya win?''

"Well, Murray, correct me if I'm wrong but weekend number one, this weekend, everyone competes under blind tasting rules. That means . . .''

"You and Murray have to be blindfolded while you eat ribs?'' You could see the idea for another performance piece germinating in Joe Long's mind.

Heaven gave him a look. "No, but all entries are presented in the same Styrofoam containers. You don't know whose brisket is whose. The last weekend is on-site judging. The judges will go around to the various smokers and the contestants really carry on with lots of barbeque decor. You know how the Que Queens wear costumes and all that shit for charity? Well, these people are gonna decorate for $100,000 in prize money. It should be wild.''

Jack looked at the assembled group through the mirror behind the bar without turning around to face them. "Most points wins?''

"You got it, Jack.'' Murray said. "Everyone will know who's ahead after the first judging this Saturday, but some people are better at on-site judging, so anything can happen that second weekend.''

Murray didn't know how right he was going to be.

Chapter 10

When Heaven arrived at the commissary, the big kitchen was abuzz with excitement. The Que Queens had just finished making and bottling their sauce, Royal Jelly.

Royal Jelly

1 cup orange juice
½ cup apple cider vinegar
½ cup juice from a jar of pickled peaches
4 pickled peaches
6–10 cloves of roasted garlic
½ cup each of honey mustard, yellow mustard, honey, and tomato ketchup.
⅛ cup Louisiana hot sauce
1 T. dried Coleman's mustard
1 T. kosher salt
1 T. ground white pepper

Combine the peaches (pitted) and the roasted garlic in the food processor and puree. Add this mix to all the other ingredients in a heavy, medium saucepan and simmer 20–30 minutes, until the sauce has thickened and turned a golden orange. Cool and refrigerate.

Alice Aron was hosing out the big freestanding stockpot where Pigpen had been found sauced on Tuesday. She waved Heaven over. Alice was the executive chef of a large hotel and because of her interest in smoke cooking, the hotel had sponsored a team. They had had a great season of competition and had made it to the World Series. Alice would be on the other side of the fence on Saturday but she was with the Queens tonight and she had news.

"You'll never guess who was here earlier," Alice taunted.

Heaven pretended she was really thinking about this. "Ollie Gates saying he wants our sauce recipe and he doesn't care how much money it costs?" Ollie Gates owned a chain of Kansas City barbeque restaurants.

"No, but sauce was the theme. Two of Pigpen's team members came out to look around. They say Pigpen has never let them be present when he makes up the sauce and has never let them see the recipe. He told them there was a copy in his bank deposit box. They asked his wife to look for it when she went to get the life insurance policy and she swears there isn't a recipe anywhere. They were fit to be tied. They couldn't very well go out and tear up the Hopkins's house looking for a damn recipe when there's grieving going on. So they came out here to tear this place apart, neatly, of course. They looked up and down, cussing the whole time. Didn't find a scrap of paper anywhere."

Stephanie and Sally Jo had just finished packing the sauce in cartons. They were now washing the parts of the bottling machine and putting it back together so Heaven could bottle the dry rub. It was easier to run the sneezy stuff through the funnel and into the long-necked bottles, just as though it were liquid.

Sally Jo looked up from the sink. "This is gonna cost that team the prize. Also, I heard they grossed about fifty thousand last year, selling their sauce at contests. That had to be some beer change for those long nights tendin' the fire."

Stephanie was refreshing her makeup from a huge stock of cosmetics she hauled around with her. "Those boys were in a serious bind tonight. The batch Pigpen was working on Tuesday was the batch for the World Series. They have no sauce."

"And, as I recall, that is the same sauce that the men's charity team, the dreaded M.C.P., uses. Yes, there is a God and She has helped Her sisters," Heaven chuckled.

"Well, this sister had better get home before the door is locked on her for the night," Sally Jo said. Sally's husband was a conservative stockbroker who could barely tolerate her involvement in something as common as barbeque contests.

Stephanie put her bottles and potions away. "Heaven, are you gonna be all right out here by yourself? It's kinda creepy after, you know, Tuesday. I'd stay but I have a shoot tomorrow and my call time is seven A.M. I have to make a ham look cute at seven in the morning."

Heaven poured a glass of wine from one of the bottles that the team had been sharing, Flora Springs barrel-fermented Chardonnay, and pushed Stephanie toward the door. Alice and Sally Jo were standing there already. "Get out, all of you."

"But it's so big here and empty and . . ." Stephanie was retreating and trying to get the last word in at the same time.

"Get. We have to have this done by tomorrow and I can still be home before midnight, which is earlier than I'd get home if I'd stayed at the cafe." Heaven waved at the three as they went out the delivery door at the back.

In an hour Heaven was almost done with her chore. She got up to sip wine and pour the last few cups of the mixture into the large funnel. She was wearing a breathing mask and as she turned to the table where the wine was, a huge crash came from the big room. The bottling machine was situated in a small tile room that was off the main kitchen. Heaven didn't have the door shut but she had been sitting with her back to the opening. There were lights on around the walls but there was also a big darkness in the middle of the room. Heaven peered out and saw at once what had caused the crash.

Down on his hands and knees under two large stockpots was the Barbeque Guild president, Paul Taylor. On the floor beside him were several big pots that had been resting, over-turned, on top of an empty dairy case, the kind that gallons of milk and quarts of cream were delivered in, a dairy case that Paul had evidently bumped. Paul certainly hadn't both-ered to say, "Howdy, Heaven, I'll be crawling around over here for a while." Heaven yelped but she forgot she had on the breathing mask so her cry made a loud humming noise that vibrated her lips. It sounded like a bad car alarm. Paul Taylor jumped and started and whacked his head on the mechanical lift on the side of the stockpot, the thing that tilted the pot over when you wanted to unload it. By this time, Heaven had ripped her mask off and could really yell. "Paul, what in the world are you doing? You scared me to death."

Paul Taylor was a tall man of six-foot-three or so. He was having a hell of a time backing himself out from under the cooking pots. There was a welt on the top of his almost-bald head. "Heaven, I didn't see you in there."

"Paul, I'd consider that an insult if I believed you. What are you doing at eleven at night examining the gas valves of the stockpots? This wasn't going to be some horrible accident where the place blows up and you collect the in-surance money, was it? Is it?" Heaven, you fool, she thought to herself. If that is what he was doing, now you'll be sure to be an innocent victim. Now that you've spelled it out so beautifully for him.

"Heaven, you have that acid wit, don't you? No, the fel-lows on Pigpen's team called. They were a little upset, feel they might have to back out of the competition if they don't find the sauce recipe. I thought maybe it got caught under the gismos down there. Told them I'd come and take a look.'' Paul was walking closer to Heaven, rubbing his head as he walked.

"The fellows on Pigpen's team have already been out here, Paul. Come to think of it, weren't you and Pigpen on the same team years ago?'' Heaven walked casually in the opposite direction.

Paul nodded. "Ten, twelve years ago. We were best buddies and helped start the Barbeque Guild. But things change, Heaven, you know that don't you?''

What was he referring to, Heaven asked herself. Her husbands? Her careers? Her haircuts? "Maybe you can help those guys out, Paul. Surely you know Pigpen's sauce recipe?''

"He always was a secretive bastard,'' Paul said in a faroff tone of voice. "He didn't share with me any more than he did with them. That's one of the reasons . . . '' Paul stopped talking.

I better wrap this up quick, Heaven thought. He's wigging out on me. The next thing I know he'll be confessing not only that he was going to blow up the building but also that he killed Pigpen.

Heaven chirped in her brightest voice, picking up the sentence where Paul had left off. "That's one of the reasons Pigpen Hopkins was a legend in the barbeque game. Paul, will you wait for me ten minutes while I finish up these last bottles of dry rub and then walk me to my car? It is getting late. Oh, and you might ask the police, they could have taken the recipe along with the other, ah, physical evidence.'' Heaven couldn't help mentally picturing Pigpen as he had looked on Tuesday, physical evidence indeed.

She shifted into high gear, pouring the rest of the powdered mixture in the funnel and pushing a bottle under the spigot. She didn't want to stay by herself and she didn't want to leave Paul there either.

"I called the police after the boys called me. They don't have the recipe.'' Paul looked at Heaven suspiciously. "I'll just wait in the office.''

As Heaven worked as fast as she could, Paul Taylor went into the small office at the front of the building. Soon Heaven could see the light on the extension phone come on, glowing red. Who was he calling? Someone to torture the recipe out of me? His wife? The Pigpen team boys?

The last bottle was done. Heaven packed it in the carton she had been filling. Quickly she took a dry towel and wiped out the funnel and other parts of the machine she could reach. The parts she couldn't reach without taking the machine apart were just going to have dry rub dust on them. She was not going to spend another minute in this creepy place. Heaven took one case of the filled bottles with her and went in the office. Paul looked up and mumbled a "good-bye" in the mouthpiece of the phone.

"Paul, I have four more of these in the back. Would you help me get them out to the car?" Heaven was pointing to the case of dry rub.

"Sure, Heaven."

In two minutes they were loading the last two cartons in Heaven's van. As she climbed behind the wheel, Paul Taylor stared intently at Heaven from outside the passenger-side window. It made Heaven's skin crawl.

"Will I see you tomorrow at the funeral?" Paul asked.

"If I can get away from the restaurant," Heaven answered. As fast as she could, Heaven started the van and pulled out of the parking lot, leaving Paul Taylor standing there, still staring.

"I hope I don't have to go back there for a long time," Heaven said out loud to herself as she looked in the rearview mirror.

Chapter 11

Heaven drove north from the suburbs, toward the Missouri River. Her neighborhood, Columbus Park, was the last parcel of land before you crossed over the river to North Kansas City. Columbus Park was the neighborhood that had always been the first place new immigrants stopped when they moved to Kansas City. It had been the first home of the Irish, the Italians and the Vietnamese. It had also been Heaven's first stop when she landed back in Kansas City.

That had been in the early seventies, when she was fleeing her rock-and-roll-star husband and the life they'd led in London. Heaven was pregnant and knew the baby didn't stand a chance in that world of wealth and drugs because she herself didn't stand a chance there. She rented a flat in Columbus Park, around the corner from the Holy Rosary Catholic Church. Her next-door neighbor, Angelo Broncato, was an elderly baker who befriended Heaven and, soon after, her baby. When Angelo died with no relatives in the United States, he left the building that had been his bakery and home to Heaven and Iris in his will.

The bakery closed when Angelo died. None of his employees could make the crusty loaves of bread like he did. Soon, Iris and Heaven moved in. The bakery had been an anchor for Heaven through all the adventures and marriages that had happened since. Eventually, she always came back to Fifth Street and the bakery. Tonight she couldn't get there fast enough.

Heaven drove downtown on I-35 and was heading for the exit on Admiral Boulevard when the car behind her turned on its brights. "What an asshole," she muttered out loud. Heaven changed lanes and the bright lights stayed right behind her, only they seemed to be speeding closer to the van. As Heaven rounded the curve on the east side of downtown Kansas City, she got the distinct feeling the asshole behind her was not just a thoughtless motorist. The headlights were bearing down and then, *blam*, the van took a less than gentle tap on its back bumper.

"Shit, this is . . ."

Blam, another hit. Heaven swung across two lanes and the headlights did the same. She made it to her exit and sped up the ramp. The headlights followed and came up on her right, trying to pull next to the van. The exit lane was narrowing and Heaven stole a glance at the offending vehicle next to her while trying not to be pushed into the guardrail. The headlights were connected to a Blazer or Jeep that was black or dark green from what she could see. It was, after all, midnight, and they were careening to their deaths. There was no time for her usual thorough investigation. At the top of the hill, the exit lane intersected with Admiral Boulevard. The traffic light was red but Heaven quickly looked right and left, and seeing no other traffic, she plowed through the light, continuing down the hill toward Independence Avenue. The Jeep did the same, creeping up on her right. Heaven stole another glance and saw the driver's window silently going down. Hoping to see who was driving, she touched the brakes to slow down a little. A large gun was all she spotted as her eyes strained toward the other car. A gun the size of a cannon, Heaven thought, as she slammed on the brakes and ducked at the same time. A bullet crashed into the passenger window. The car and its driver cut in front of Heaven's van and kept going. Heaven peeked up from the huddle she was in, fully expecting to

see her would-be killer get out of the car and head her way
with that bazooka. Instead she saw the wagon hit the bottom
of the hill and speed off to the east. Heaven turned off the
van and sat there panting. She looked at her hands and legs.
She felt her face. Blood was gushing from somewhere. "Am
I shot?" Heaven asked herself. Her fingers found a piece of
glass jutting from her temple. "Oh, thank God. I'm just cut.
I'm alive and going to be sick," Heaven murmured out loud.
The thought of a piece of glass stuck in her head just a half-
inch shy of her eye sent a wave of dizziness over her. She
opened her door to let some fresh air in. As she did, a police
patrol car pulled up behind her, probably because the van
was perched halfway down an exit ramp.

"Any trouble?" the patrolman called as he got out of his
car.

"Plenty," Heaven answered. Then she fainted.

Chapter 12

"Just keep your head between your legs. Try to relax. Breathe deep," the policeman was saying in a soothing voice. Heaven could see his young face over her, slightly out of focus. She was propped up by the side of the van, sitting smack dab on the street with her hero's hand on the back of her neck, folding her forward. "The ambulance is on the way. Don't you worry," he cooed as he glanced over his shoulder. Heaven realized that there were now two patrol cars behind the van, the second one carrying two other of-ficers, both women. One was on the radio and the other was pacing.

"I'm fine. Don't need an ambulance," Heaven said as she attempted to get to her feet. The attempt failed and she sank down to the pavement again. "Whoa, I'm still dizzy. And still bleeding, I guess," she said as she touched her face and shirt. By this time, the blood had soaked Heaven's T-shirt and made her neck a sticky mess.

The patrolman who had discovered Heaven nodded. "You need some stitches. But I couldn't, ah, I didn't, eh, I don't think you have any other wounds." He looked em-barrassed at having to confess to a physical search of an unconscious woman, no matter how justified. "From the looks of your window, I'm guessing someone shot at you. Am I right?"

Heaven rested her head against the side of the car and

closed her eyes. The world started spinning. Closing my eyes was a mistake, she thought as she opened them quickly and tried to focus on the question and the face asking it. "A Jeep or Blazer came up behind me and bumped me and when I got off the highway, they followed. They rolled down the window and this big gun stuck out and . . . I think only one shot, then they ran away."

Heaven had started out this speech believing she could describe everything that had happened in detail but she ran out of steam. It was too hard to think right now. "Will you please have them take me to K.U. Med Center? My boyfriend is working tonight. . . . I think he's working . . ." Heaven heard the siren and suddenly felt silly. Confused and silly. She got up. "Can't I just drive myself? I'm cut, not killed, and I'll feel like a fool riding in that thing. Who'll drive my car?"

"Sorry. I'm going to tow it so the evidence guys can give it a look-see. Hopefully we'll find the shell that will convict whoever did this," her new police friend said. "You'll be fine but head wounds bleed a lot and you are not about to drive yourself to the emergency room. Hold on and don't argue." He steered her toward the ambulance.

Three plus hours later, at a mere four in the morning, Heaven and Hank were headed back to Fifth Street together in Hank's car.

Hank was a mess. He totally lost it when Heaven showed up in the ambulance, bloody from head to toe, with a piece of glass jutting out of her temple. He got off duty as fast as someone could get in to replace him. He peered over the shoulder of the plastic surgeon on call who did the honors on Heaven's face. He conferred with the police, the doctors and Detective Bonnie Weber by phone.

Heaven had asked the patrolman, her new best friend, to call Bonnie when they got to the hospital. Bonnie had been asleep but she roused herself and talked to the patrolman, the doctor, Heaven and Hank. None of this made Hank feel better.

Now, as they neared Fifth Street, Hank reached over to the passenger seat and touched Heaven on the cheek. He lifted his hand up to the stitches. They reached from Heaven's eyebrow to her hairline. They were ugly but could be hidden by her hair, although only barely, because of the new haircut.

"The Doc did a good job," Hank said in a worried voice.

Heaven smiled weakly. "He didn't have a choice. You were like a little old lady, hovering and clucking. You practically kissed his shoes."

Hank looked straight at Heaven. "I thanked him for coming in, for his expertise. From one doctor to another. I had a lot at stake. My heart . . ."

Heaven closed her eyes and held his hand tight against her. "Belongs to me. Just a little longer."

"Your timetable, not mine. I'm here for the duration. Heaven, can we go back to the incident tonight? I . . ."

"We're home. Wait till we get in the house and in bed. Then I'll answer anything. Just let me get these disgusting clothes off and shower the hospital away." Hank hopped out and opened the garage door at Heaven's. She had built a garage over the parking lot Angelo had used for his bakery customers. There was a garage entrance into the building so Heaven didn't have to go outside when she got home late at night or early in the morning. Heaven also had an automatic garage-door opener but the gadget was in her van, not Hank's Honda.

She and Hank moved inside, walking through the big kitchen/dining room/living room where Heaven had had her catering business before owning the restaurant. It was also where Heaven entertained and where people hung out when they came to visit. There was a full industrial-strength kitchen with ranges and convection ovens and hoods. The old coal ovens that had made Angelo's bread the best in the city were still in the walls. Baskets and platters were stacked on baker's racks. Heaven wanted the first floor to always have something of Angelo and the bakery in it.

Upstairs she had created her own aura. The second-floor living quarters had been changed a great deal. Many tiny rooms had evolved into four big ones: a sitting room/studio where Heaven wrote and worked on menus and read, a bedroom, a huge bathroom, and Iris's bedroom and studio. Heaven was a collector and the place was full of her various interests: antique photographs, quilts, a prize jukebox. Hank always said he learned all about America in Heaven's home.

Hank's real name was Huy Wing. He had been born in Vietnam and had escaped in the nick of time twenty-one years before, at age four. He and his mother and sister had arrived in Columbus Park with very little money and few possessions. Hank's father had been executed for working for the Americans just a week before they left their country. Now his sister was at M.I.T. and Hank was a doctor. His mother still lived around the corner from Heaven in the first apartment the Wings had occupied in their new city. Hank still lived there too, although he spent more and more time at Heaven's as the months wore on. They had been seeing each other for a year now, but it didn't start just a year ago. Hank had fallen in love with Heaven when he was seventeen. They had known each other from a distance for years. On the day her most recent husband, Jason Kelley, moved out last year, Hank had spotted the moving van and celebrated privately. A few days later, he went to Heaven's door and asked for cooking lessons. Heaven laughed and told him he would have to teach her Viet cuisine if she was going to teach him American. They cooked together once a week for a while. And then twice a week. It was somewhere around the third week that Hank got up enough nerve to kiss Heaven. Their worlds had both changed with that kiss. Tonight Hank had been flooded with memories as he remembered every kiss since then. He was watching Heaven take a shower, watching for fear she would faint or get her stitches wet. Their eyes met through the shower fog and Heaven stuck out her tongue at him, rolling her eyes like he was being an overprotective parent. She cut off the water and stepped out, shaking her head and sending water flying on Hank.

"Don't get your stitches wet," Hank said as he grabbed a towel and started drying Heaven's face carefully. "Heaven, I need to know if you think the barbeque guy was responsible for the shot fired at you. You sounded like he was for a minute when you were talking to Bonnie Weber on the phone but then you downplayed it with the other cops. What's the story?"

Heaven pulled on a huge T-shirt that said Kansas City Chiefs on the front and jumped into bed. "All I know is this guy was acting weird, crawling around on the floor out at the commissary tonight looking for a secret recipe, then he goes into the office and calls someone, then he hangs up quick when I come into the room, then I get shot at. Probably no connection. I was probably just in the way of a psycho but . . ." Heaven's voice had trailed off almost the minute her head hit the pillow. It could have had something to do with the tranquilizer the doctor had given her. Hank held her hand tightly till dawn, a time that came sooner than either one of them wanted it to.

Chapter 13

The church was almost full. For a disagreeable creep, Pig-pen Hopkins sure had a good draw at his last rites. Heaven slipped in the back of the sanctuary and stood up against the wall, trying to get the lay of the land. The crowd and church seemed to be divided into two camps, one side of barbeque team members and one side of family members and devotees of Pigpen's plumbing skills. Detective Bonnie Weber was there, as well as several men who had to be involved in law enforcement. Their quaint wardrobes elim-inated them from the other categories. Heaven herself had a hard time figuring out what to wear. She was well stocked in black clothes, but somehow she didn't see her usual Gap T-shirt and tights as appropriate funeral attire. She settled on a snappy black silk dress and a loose black double-breasted leather jacket. Heaven took a seat at the back of the family-member side so she could get a better look at the barbeque side.

Most of the faces were familiar. Even though Heaven wasn't a true cooker, she had been on the fringes of the contests for several years. Because barbeque contests were growing as a sport and competition, there were new faces every year. Heaven suspected that today most of the people she didn't know were from out of town. The team of big boys, for instance, sitting down four rows. It didn't take a detective to know they were the Nashville Nine. Their matching shiny nylon jackets gave it away in script letters on their broad backs. And even as Heaven was checking out the crowd, a new group came in and greeted almost everyone on the barbeque side of the church. Leading this new contingent was the biggest black man Heaven had ever laid eyes on off the football field, of course. He must have been six-eight with hands the size of hams. Everyone seemed to know him and he went over to Mrs. Hopkins like an old friend, giving her a hug that lifted her from the church pew. Heaven couldn't help herself. She looked over at Detective Bonnie Weber and jerked her head in Goliath's direction. Bonnie gave her a look that seemed more focused on Heaven's stitches, a look that asked, "What are you doing here?" The service began.

In forty minutes, they all stood up to file out to the strains of that old Methodist standby, "The Garden," and Bonnie and Heaven made a beeline for each other in the back of the church. They both wanted to get the first word in. Bonnie won.

"What are you doing here? In fact, what are you doing anywhere? You should be home for God's sake. How do you feel?" Bonnie said gruffly.

Heaven stomped her foot. "Hello, Detective? Someone killed Pigpen on Tuesday and shot at me on Thursday. He was at the sauce-making capital of Kansas City when he died and I had just left there when I was target practice. Call me paranoid, but I'm afraid this might not be coincidence. I came to see who showed up and . . ."

Just then, Stephanie Simpson burst in on the twosome. She had come from outdoors.

"Stephanie, you're late. The service is over," Heaven said, trying to turn her head away from Stephanie to shield the side with the damage.

Stephanie was practically jumping with excitement. "I know, I know. I was a little late and when I got here the caravan was forming in front and I got busy meeting people and the next thing I know you were all streaming out of the church. Heaven, what in the hell is the matter with your head, girl? God, those are stitches! What happened?''

Heaven looked out the front door. ''I'll tell you on the way to the cemetery. Will you ride with me? I have Hank's car today. I dropped him off at the hospital. Don't ask, I'll explain that too. Bonnie, why don't you come with us? And, Steph, what are you talking about, what caravan?''

By the time Stephanie could open her mouth to answer, she didn't have to. The trio had reached the door of the church and could see for themselves. Outside the church were dozens of barbeque cookers, (the people), with their smokers, (the pieces of equipment), and Winnebagos and campers and pickups. The colorful parade would follow the hearse to the cemetery. Pickups trailing flatbeds with elaborate smoking devices lined up like homecoming floats. Vintage panel trucks had team names painted on the side like ''The Slaughterhouse Gang'' and ''Pigs in a Poke.'' Some of the slickest rigs in the country were ready to accompany Pigpen on his final trip.

The one Heaven couldn't take her eyes off of was the one leading the pack. It was an authentic Western chuck wagon pulled by a team of eight mules. A mule team that somehow had driven into the depths of Kansas City. A mule team that was causing the traffic cops assigned to this funeral to consult their superiors on motorcycle radios. A mule team under the control of one of the most handsome men in America, Bo Morales. Heaven had read about him and seen his photo. But seeing him in all his live extravagance was something else. He was wearing one of those Australian longcoats, the ankle-length duster kind with the cape over the shoulders. He had jet-black shoulder-length hair and blue eyes only Paul Newman could top. As they watched he laughed, standing up on his wagon to yell at his mule team in Spanish. It was a sight to behold.

The three women were speechless for a brief moment. Then Bonnie Weber found her voice. ''Whoa, baby. I can see why you didn't come inside, Stephanie. I know I should go help those poor traffics with this nightmare but I need a little more time to ogle.''

Stephanie nodded. ''Bo is one of the front-runners in the World Series this year. He won ten major competitions in Texas and something at Memphis in May. And he does it all with authentic 1880 equipment, nothing modern like Coleman coolers.''

Heaven eyed her friend suspiciously. ''Stephanie, how do you know so much about Bo Morales?''

Stephanie tried looking coy. ''Well, after all, I am a food stylist. Even if he was ugly as sin and came driving up in that getup, I'd be interested. I went over and introduced myself. He was very nice and said to stop by his camp and he'd show me how his equipment works.''

''Right,'' Heaven and Bonnie said more or less at the same time.

Stephanie flounced. ''You two know what I mean. Where's your car, Heaven? Detective, are you coming with us?''

Bonnie shook her head. ''No way. I'm working here. I wish you two would go back to your lives. You can't tell me you just had to come to this funeral because of your deep, abiding respect for the deceased. Your noses are very close to my business. Heaven, you're in no shape . . .''

''Forget it,'' Heaven said firmly. ''I was going to do this before I knew it was a Fellini movie with a gorgeous cowboy involved. I'm sure not going home now. My face won't feel any better at home. I don't have to be at the restaurant because Brian is back from, eh, an infraction. I want to see this circus parade firsthand.''

With that parting salvo, Heaven and Stephanie jumped in Hank's car to get in line for the funeral procession.

Chapter 14

The trip to the cemetery was priceless. Needless to say, no one else at the Englewood Memorial Gardens in Independence, Missouri, had ever had a procession like Pigpen Hopkins's, whose real name, it was announced more than once, was Dewayne. The trailers and smokers were parked and the crowd spilled out around the markers and family-plot stones.

Heaven and Stephanie hung back, not wanting to take up valuable space in the grieving tent. As the cooking teams assembled around the gravesite, Heaven felt that chill that comes when someone is staring at you. She looked around and saw Paul Taylor. He turned quickly away from Heaven and back toward the minister. Heaven punched Stephanie and pointed at Paul, not raising her hand.

"I saw him looking up here. He is being scary," Stephanie murmured without opening her mouth. "I heard he didn't want to be the sixth pallbearer but the other officers of the guild said he had to or it would look bad. After all, Pigpen's team only has five members left and Paul used to be on that team. He was the natural choice. This is too weird. Paul has always been so nice. You don't think he had anything to do with the drive-by, do you?"

Heaven's eyes were scanning the crowd while a cooking team, The Barbershop Bones, sang. The "Bones" not only competed in barbeque contests, but also in barbershop-quartet meets. She suddenly realized why nothing rang a bell. "I should be looking at the cars, not the faces. Cover for me, I'm going to sashay down the gravel path we came in on," Heaven whispered to Stephanie. She quickly walked back toward the place where Hank's car was parked, looking for a dark Jeep in the process. Although the preferred method of transportation for barbeque contest people was the pick-up truck, there were plenty of vans and four-wheel-drive vehicles. Heaven saw three dark Jeeps and one black Blazer. She was making her way to the nearest Jeep when the whinny of livestock caught her by surprise. "Oh, dear, I've wandered too close to the chuck wagon," she said out loud in her worst Southern accent.

A voice as smooth as silk called out, "I don't bite."

Heaven walked around to the front of the wagon and found herself face-to-face with Bo Morales in the flesh. He was feeding his mules oats to distract them from what they really wanted to eat, the artificial flowers decorating various gravesites. He was also smiling at Heaven and now that she was close enough, he stuck out his hand. Heaven took it in both of hers and wished for one second that she didn't make her living putting her hands in vats of boiling oil, burning hot ovens, sinks full of bleach and water. She paused a beat and then released his hand and smiled back. "You are Bo Morales, straight from Amarillo. And I'm Heaven Lee. I own a cafe here in Kansas City and I'm judging this weekend, among other things."

Bo tilted his head back and laughed, a very disconcerting move to Heaven. "So that's why I've never seen you before. I know if you were a cooker, I'd remember you. Of that you can be sure," Bo pulled a single yellow rose from behind his back and presented it to Heaven with a flourish. She gulped.

"Something tells me I've seen this rose before. Could it have been on that lovely yellow floral display on top of Pigpen's coffin?" Heaven teased.

"Live flowers are for the living, I always say."

Heaven remembered she was investigating. "Why aren't you over there, singing "Amazing Grace" with the rest of them?"

Bo tilted and laughed again. "Enough is enough. I made this parade out of respect to barbeque, not the idiot we're here to bury. Most of the team members from around the country know that Pigpen was not a shining example of the sport."

"Well, then, it was very nice of you all to show up," Heaven said.

"That's the kind of folks we are, ma'am." Bo was really laying it on thick. Heaven hated being called ma'am. Thank God he made a tiny mistake, she thought.

Just as Heaven was trying to drag herself away from Bo Morales and over to the dark Jeep a few feet away, a piercing scream came from the direction of the gravesite. Bo grabbed her arm for just an instant to turn her around, then they both ran toward the noise. Heaven got there after Bo but in plenty of time to see what had caused the disruption.

It was time to remove the casket from the hearse for its last short journey, and the funeral home director opened the back door of the limo only to find Paul Taylor, Barbeque Guild president, leaning over from the driver's seat and peering into the now-open casket of Pigpen Hopkins. Paul hadn't been visible before because of the tinted windshields that hid the coffin from public view. It didn't appear as though Paul just needed a last look. He seemed to be going through the pockets of the deceased. Mrs. Pigpen had chosen to bury her beloved in his favorite plumbing outfit, a pair of blue denim bib overalls with the words PIGPEN PLUMBING printed on the bib. Paul's rather large right hand had gotten stuck in one of the pockets on that front bib, and when he had been discovered, he jumped, trying to get his hand out quickly. The jump caused the lid of the coffin to shut halfway and Paul was caught with his paw in the cookie jar, so to speak. The funeral director yelped with surprise and this caught the attention of the whole audience. Mrs.

Pigpen, sensing something was amiss, rose from her chair and made her way closer to the hearse. That was where the first scream had come in. The screams and yelps continued as the widow and her brother, a partner in the plumbing business, tried to pull Paul Taylor out of the front of the car by force.

"Help me get my damn hand out," Paul was saying.

"This is unprecedented," the funeral director was saying.

"I'll help you, you son of a bitch, you always did hate Dewayne," Mrs. Hopkins was bellowing.

It was hard to keep a straight face, and a lot of the crowd was chuckling softly, softly out of respect for the occasion. Heaven circled around to get a better look just as Paul Taylor backed out of the hearse with the two Pigpen survivors attached to him, cursing and pulling. She thought she saw Paul pushing a crumpled piece of paper into his coat pocket. But she didn't have time for reflection or inspection when the whole ball of people fell her way. Paul Taylor grabbed at Heaven to keep his balance. She almost went over but caught herself by grabbing at Mrs. Hopkins. Finally, two or three of the pallbearers grabbed Paul Taylor and took him away. Heaven didn't know whether to laugh or to cry as she straightened herself up and went to look for her friends. She turned around and almost ran over Bonnie Weber, who was writing on her legal pad as fast as she could.

"No one will ever believe me," the detective muttered with a chuckle, shaking her head.

Chapter 15

The kitchen of Cafe Heaven was abuzz with activity. The day crew and the night crew were passing the torch. Of course, Brian Hoffman was on both the day and the night crew. It was his first day back on the job and Heaven had asked him to work for her so she could go to the barbeque contest and help the Que Queens get set up. Brian had wisely said he'd be glad to. Even though they weren't in the official competition, the Queens wanted to be at the six-thirty cooks' meeting.

Rules and regulations weren't the only thing Heaven was hoping to get at that meeting. She was also hoping for more scoop on Paul Taylor and the embarrassing events of this morning. Heaven had come in after the funeral at about two-thirty, and she had worked hard to help get the prep done for tonight. Having a big food contest in town had generated lots of out-of-towners. People from all over the country came along to root for their favorite teams. Out-of-towners ate out, so the restaurant had lots of reservations for both Friday and Saturday night.

Heaven was almost ready to leave. She had talked to the front of the house and had packed up her knives. She still brought her own personal favorite knives back and forth with her every day, just like most practicing cooks. She also had a service bring sharpened knives to the restaurant twice a month and take away the dull knives. She didn't insist that cooks have their own knives but everyone cooking at the cafe usually either had them or got them. Heaven stuck her own knife bag under her arm and suddenly smiled her best smile. Hank had just come in the back door. He smiled back and reached out to check Heaven's face. "How does it feel?" he asked.

Heaven hugged him. "It's sore. It gives me a throbbing headache but aspirin helps."

"I got your van for you," Hank said.

"You're kidding. What a guy. How did you pull that one off?"

Hank shrugged. "I asked the officer to please call me when the van could be picked up. I told him I didn't want you to see it until I'd had a chance to replace the window. I imagined it would be upsetting for you to see it that way, all broken and everything. They recovered a slug from a .44-caliber gun, I think that's the number."

The whole kitchen was silent for a minute. No one did nice things like that anymore, you could practically hear everyone thinking. Brian broke the spell with, "Man, you're a good dude."

Hank blushed and so did Heaven. They went out in the alley and traded car keys. Heaven put both hands on the new passenger window and planted a big kiss on it. "Hank, you're the best. How can I ever repay you?"

"Well, I'll be home by midnight. We could talk about a payment plan then."

Heaven unlocked the van and jumped in. "It's a date." She was off to the Bottoms.

The World Series of Barbeque was going to be held in the same place the famous American Royal Barbeque Contest was held, the West Bottoms. In the old days, the river bottoms had housed the Kansas City stockyards and miles of narrow wooden chutes that had led many a good steer to its demise. The stockyards were gone now but Kemper Arena stood in its place, ready to entertain with rock shows and rodeos, and, once a year, a great livestock show, the

American Royal. One American Royal show awarded prizes for growing the best pig or steer or sheep. The other American Royal contest awarded prizes for cooking the same.

It was the parking lot of this arena that became the temporary home of this peculiar World Series with its hundreds of people, scores of Porta Pottis, and dozens of beer and ice and meat trucks. On Saturday it would also see thousands of visitors who would come to buy T-shirts and barbeque sauce and dry rub and maybe get a bite of some prizewinning barbeque. The health department frowned on giving away samples, and there was perfectly good barbeque for sale by local restaurants. But everyone wanted to taste the ribs of the champs.

Heaven pulled into the parking lot, madly pawing through the mail on the floor of the van for her parking pass. She found it in an envelope along with a plastic wristband that had "All Access" printed on it and a judge's badge. The attendant let her pass, and she parked quickly and ran into the livestock exhibition building in back of the main arena. The cooking teams were sitting around tables in a large hall that was empty except for the tables and chairs that would be used tomorrow for the judging. An officer of the Kansas City Barbeque Guild was standing in front of the crowd. Paul Taylor was nowhere in sight. Heaven spotted Meridith and Sally Jo and sat down beside them just as the speaker began. Bonnie Weber was over in a corner.

"I want to welcome you all to the second World Series of Barbeque. Our guild president, Paul Taylor, is not feeling well and couldn't be here tonight." There was a ripple of laughter through the crowd. The guild officer shifted uncomfortably but continued, "As you know, this contest is not run by the Kansas City rules or the international rules or the Memphis rules but by a mixture of all of them, so be sure to ask a field captain if you're not sure about something. We don't want anyone disqualified because they didn't know what a rule was. As you have seen, we have refrigerator trucks out on the field. As you checked in, we asked you to check your meat at the nearest meat truck. Your meat was inspected to make sure it was raw, not in a marinade or pre-cooked. It was then left exactly as you gave it to us, in coolers with your team name on 'em. There is a security guard at every meat truck. No one can tamper with your meat." Another ripple of laughter went through the crowd. "Unless she's pretty," someone yelled. The official pushed on. "You may check out your contest meat after eleven tonight. Field captains may come by your camp and ask to inspect your meat at any time after that. The first item, as you can see by your schedule, is due at this judges' area by noon tomorrow. I believe the first item to be judged is sausage. You all are experienced or you wouldn't be here. You have your rules and regulations in your booklet. Any questions?"

From the back of the room, a booming voice called out, "Where's the beer?"

As everyone in the room laughed and you could feel tension relax, Heaven turned to see that the voice belonged to the big black man from the funeral.

The guild official smiled and answered, "In the Board of Trade tent at eight o'clock. They're giving a reception for all the teams and judges. That gives you enough time to finish your setup, so let's go to work. Good luck everyone."

Heaven and her teammates followed the crowd out the side door to the parking lot full of activity. "That was sure a non-event. Who was that guy and what have they done with Paul? Taken him to the place where the quiet people go?" Heaven asked.

Sally Jo shrugged. "No one knows where he is but everyone knows what happened at the funeral. What class, rolling a stiff right in front of God and the widow. The whole village is hopping with bits and pieces of gossip, like that someone took a shot at you last night. Why didn't you call with this info yourself, young lady?"

Heaven's hand went up to her temple involuntarily.

Sally Jo's eyes doubled in size as she took in Heaven's wound. "You were shot! No one said you'd been shot. Oh my God."

"I have not been shot. The window of the van was shot out and a piece of glass came flying across the car and stuck in my head, that's all."

"Well, that's not what I heard." This came from Barbara, who was flat on her back underneath the trailer that carried her smoker.

The women had arrived at the site of the Battle of the Sexes Cook-off. They were situated in front of the actual World Series contestant sites, closer to the stage where bands would play tomorrow and close to the funnel-cake wagon and soft-drink booth. This location was chosen to attract more paying customers to the contest and make more money for the Food Bank.

Laughter erupted from under the trailer. "Yes, I heard you and Paul Taylor were having a mad affair and you broke up with him last night and his erratic behavior is all your fault. He's a victim of a broken heart. It's made him lose his mind."

"Oh, brother. You're making this up, you goof," Heaven kicked at Barbara's boot. Barbara shimmied out from under her trailer. "I was just placing the balances to make our playing field level. We don't want any hot spots inside the cooker."

Barbara had devised a group of wooden wedges that she placed under the wheels when the smoker wasn't on perfectly flat ground, which it wasn't at most contests. She placed a level on the smoker and smiled. "Now, that's more like it. We can fire her up now."

"I'll do that," Heaven said. She went to the firebox end of the smoker and looked on the side in the wood holder. "What should we use? I feel like an apple and cherry combination." She started building a fire with hardwood lump charcoal and oak logs, topped with apple and cherry logs. As Heaven did this, the other team members present, Sally

Jo, Meridith and Barbara, continued to make camp. Not that it was that primitive. Barbara owned a Winnebago, so no one had to sleep outside. Tonight Barbara and Meridith would spend the night to tend the fire. Sally Jo was not allowed by Mr. Barton to stay all night at these affairs. Next week it would be Heaven and Stephanie's turn.

The Que Queens had set up their site like most teams did, with their camper along the back of their designated area, and the smoker at right angles to the Winnebago. This created an L-shaped campsite. Meridith and Sally Jo were erecting a room-size canvas canopy in the middle of their area to create a sheltered place to sit and a cover for their worktable. The canopy was pink-and-white striped canvas with a tall pole in the middle and corner poles that had sandbags attached. It wouldn't stand up to a Kansas tornado, but it did protect the team from rain and sun, two irritations of cooking outside. Right now, however, it was pitch dark and dry, no rain or sun to bother with. Barbara was hanging a string of industrial work lights on the plug box that was attached to the generator on the side of the Winnebago. The parking lot was well lit too, but Barbara needed to get up close and personal with her ribs later and that took light.

Soon the campsite looked like it had been there for years, or at least days. Folding chairs were set around a plastic patio table and an eight-foot worktable had also been set up. A boom box was serenading the girls with old Rolling Stones tunes. The wooden and plastic crates that held bleach and soap and spices and paper towels were unloaded and the necessities were arranged neatly on the worktable. Tongs and spoons and spatulas were lined up. A restaurant-size tube of foil and one of clear plastic film were sitting on the side of the smoker. The worktable itself was covered with a colorful flowered oilcloth that Heaven had brought back from Mexico.

"We're set up. It's time for a drink," Heaven announced.

"It's time for a drink on the tab of those big-time grain

traders, I say." Barbara cracked. "Heaven, check your fire, honey, and let's go."

Heaven opened the firebox on the side of the smoker. The fire was raging. "We've got combustion going on here, folks. It's hot. The gauge is hovering around five hundred degrees."

"Good, in three hours it should be just about right. Who wants to stay? I promise I'll come back in thirty minutes and relieve whoever."

Meridith plopped down in a lawn chair. "I'll stay because I'm here all night. Sally Jo better go to the party now or she'll turn into a pumpkin."

"Let's check out the big-time players," Sally Jo said and the team walked down the aisles made by the other cookers and their smokers and campers and tables and tents. The air was filled with the smell of hardwood fires and autumn. It was chilly.

"So, Barbara, fill us in. We who only dabble in this great sport need to know who to watch tomorrow," Heaven said.

Barbara stopped in front of a block-long tent. A country band was tuning up near the front opening. There must have been three hundred people inside already. "Well, one thing you already know is that cookers don't turn down a free drink. This will be the perfect place to see all the contenders."

Suddenly Detective Bonnie Weber appeared out of nowhere. "That was my thought too. It will be a perfect place to see all the contenders for number one suspect. Ladies, don't cramp my style," she said out of the side of her mouth as she fell in beside a group of cookers from Texas who were in identical red, white and blue cowboy shirts.

The band began to play. The party had begun.

Chapter 16

Everywhere Heaven looked, there were people staring at her. Or maybe it just seemed that way because she had stitches on her temple. She grabbed Sally Jo's arm. "Are people staring at me?" she asked.

Sally Jo pushed her away playfully. "Yes, you hussy. Get a grip, girl. By now most people have heard about what happened to you last night. Whether they think it was a common drive-by shooting or that you stole Pigpen's recipe and fled, you are news, H."

"Stole his recipe? Now where did that come from?"

Barbara joined in. "A cooking team from southern Missouri told me that one, I believe. Now pay attention, kids. Approaching us on the right is one of the four teams believed to have a good shot at the crown."

Heading toward them was a beautiful tall blond woman with long wavy hair curving down over one eye, à la Rita Hayworth. Behind her trailed an all-female entourage that included a black woman even taller than the blonde. The black woman had a Grace Jones look and an aura of danger about her. The blonde turned and whispered something in her ear and Grace smiled wickedly. Now the blonde waved coyly at Barbara and stopped her promenade.

Barbara hugged the blonde superficially. "Welcome to Kansas City. Everyone, I'd like to present Felicity June Morgan, the best barbeque cooker on the eastern seaboard.

Felicity is from Savannah, or is it Charleston?''

"Oh, baby, those are fightin' words," Felicity purred as she grabbed Barbara's collar and shook her gently. "Charleston, South Carolina, home of that great pulled pork with mustard sauce. Y'all know about our pulled pork, don't ya?" she said eyeing Sally Jo and Heaven. "Who are your little friends, Barbara?"

Barbara waved her hand at her teammates. "Sally Jo Barton, Heaven Lee. Sally Jo and Heaven are on a charity cooking team with me. Sally Jo is a food editor and Heaven owns a restaurant."

Felicity circled the three women like a hungry cat. The Grace Jones look-alike was not amused. Heaven felt like an appetizer.

Felicity took a pull from her long-neck bottle of beer. "Well, well, well. This is going to be a fun weekend, a real fun weekend. Barbara, I'm sorry you didn't make it to the playoffs. Next year, baby. Ladies, we *will* see each other again." She and her merry band rolled on in formation, Felicity first, Grace Jones next, the peons bringing up the rear.

Sally Jo looked like she had swallowed her tongue. "Were, is, does Felicity . . ."

Heaven laughed. "Does Felicity like girls? Is she a lesbian? Is that what you're trying to inquire about?"

Barbara nodded. "Yes, folks, even in this wacky world of barbeque there are alternative lifestyles. The tall zombie is her girlfriend of many years. All the good old boys are scared to death of her."

Heaven rubbed her hands together. "Boy, oh boy, who's next, Barb? This is fun."

Barbara steered them across the tent toward the biggest bar, the one with twenty different beers on tap. "It's time to meet Aza. For my money, he's the favorite." They stopped in front of the black man the size of a tank. He swung Barbara up in the air the way he had swung Mrs. Hopkins at the funeral. Then he turned toward Heaven and stuck out one of those ham hands. "Eleazar Martin, at your service."

Heaven grabbed on to as many of Eleazar's digits as she could fit her hand around. "Glad to meet you. Where are you from?"

Aza Martin threw his arms around Heaven and Barbara. "From the barbeque capital of the world. Memphis, Tennessee, ladies."

Barbara punched feebly at Aza's midsection. "That's blasphemy, Aza, here in Kansas City. Heaven, Sally Jo, Aza owns one of the best and busiest barbeque chains in Memphis."

Heaven was suddenly interested. "You know, Aza, I've always wondered why the great barbeque restaurants in Kansas City don't compete. Hotels and casinos have teams, but the real-deal guys don't. What made you decide to do the circuit?"

"Well, there are a couple of things to consider here, ladies. First, if you make your living smoking meat, you sure don't want to be showed up by some plumber, God rest his soul, now do you? No, suh. Second, how many barbeque teams do you see in this room that are black?"

They all looked around the tent in vain.

Aza wagged his finger. "Nah, we don't count Felicity's main squeeze. You want to know why I'm the only black team in the top fifty? Because black people first made barbeque to eat because they were hungry, not for some damn recreation. Then if they were good at it, maybe they made it for the people in their neighborhood to buy on Sundays, which maybe turned into a seven-day-a-week cafe. Nowadays the greatest barbeque joints in the world are black owned. But do you think black folks are gonna spend their own money buyin' a bunch of fancy equipment and travel around the country to cook so they can win a big ol' aluminium trophy? This barbeque contest circuit, ladies, is a classic case of 'white folks sure is strange.' "

Heaven loved this man. "Then what made you decide to

go around the country with a bunch of fancy equipment to get those big old trophies with these crazy white folks?''

Aza grinned. ''Well, now, in the past couple of years things have changed considerably. The thing that's changed is the amount of money involved. Yes, suh. When the prizes were a couple hundred dollars, no black person would be bothered with this shit. But with a total prize pot of a hundred grand, now that got my interest, ladies. And speaking of that pot, if I'm gonna take the lion's share of it back to Memphis, I best be getting back to my rig.'' Aza shook everyone's hand again, grabbed a huge cup of beer and took off.

Heaven pulled on Barbara's jean jacket eagerly. ''Who's next on your top four list?''

''I think you met him at the funeral. Bo Morales from Texas has a good chance to win with his chuck wagon and his mules,'' Barbara said.

''Did I hear my name?'' All of a sudden Bo Morales was by Heaven's side, holding a platter of sandwiches in his hand that he had just stolen from a waiter who was supposed to be refilling the food table.

Heaven took a turkey and brie on an egg roll. ''You are certainly good at recycling, first the funeral flowers, now the catering food. Barbara here tells me you're good at cooking too.''

Bo kissed Barbara on the cheek and handed her a sandwich. ''Thanks for the good PR. Time will tell, won't it? I hope you will all come by the wagon tomorrow. Heaven, I would love to show you how everything works. It is different from your modern smoking rigs.''

Heaven blushed. ''I wouldn't miss it for the world.''

''Perhaps I could start showing you tonight?''

Sally Jo wedged in between Heaven and Bo. ''Oh, no, Mr. Morales. We have lots of work to do tonight. I'm sure you do too so we'll be seeing you tomorrow.'' She swept Heaven away with a firm guiding hand on Heaven's elbow and the stern look of a sorority housemother.

"Please, call me Bo," he called as they hustled off.

"Who's number four on your hit parade, Barbara? Isn't there anyone from Kansas City who can win this thing?" Heaven asked.

Barbara sounded unsure when she answered. "Pigpen and his team were in my top four but now no one knows what will happen. The boys look pretty glum, don't they?"

Four of the five remaining members of Pigpen's prize-winning barbeque team were lined up at the bar that served real liquor. They were all tilting in slightly different directions and seemed to have gotten their money's worth out of the free party the grain traders were giving.

"I hope they can cook intoxicated" Sally Jo said.

Barbara headed for the door. "Oh, believe me, it's how they perform best."

Bonnie Weber joined the girls at the exit.

"What have you learned?" Heaven asked her friend.

"I learned that you and Paul were having a torrid affair and that you stole the recipe and were shot at by a Vietnamese gang and . . ."

Heaven grabbed the detective's arm. "Give me a fuckin' break."

Bonnie smiled. "I would if you would just stop landing in the middle of these annoying murders."

As Heaven and her friends headed out into the night, a loud yell came from one of Pigpen's former teammates, the only one not downing a shot of tequila at the time. "Hey, Que Queens. Give us back our goddamn recipe. Hey, I mean it."

The Queens and Bonnie made a swift exit. As they hurried back to their camper, Heaven recalled how people had stared when they first arrived. She had been so caught up in Felicity and Aza and Bo she had forgotten all the nonsense about the lost recipe. "Why us?" she wondered out loud.

Barbara went first. "That's not hard. We, I mean you and Stephanie, found the dead body at the commissary."

Sally Jo continued. "Then we were out there again when those boys came looking for the recipe and when you caught Paul crawling around. Then you got shot at. We are right in the middle of this, Heaven, whether we mean to be or not. Shit, it's late. I've got to go home."

Bonnie Weber checked her watch. "Me too. I'm glad someone realizes what a mess you're in. I have to go to a weekend seminar, something about getting in touch with our collective frustration as law-enforcement personnel. I'll be back Sunday afternoon. Try not to get into trouble while I'm gone, ladies."

Barbara hugged Stephanie and Heaven. "I'll see you two in the morning. I'm gonna put the brisket and pork shoulder on about midnight and the ribs about five. If you two get here by seven in the morning, you can take over for a couple of hours. H, do you have to go back to the restaurant?"

"No, not tonight. I should but I'm just going to . . . to spend a little time with Hank."

Back at the campsite, everyone told Meridith something about the party, then Sally Jo and Heaven took off for their cars. Soon Heaven was pulling into the garage on Fifth Street. Her stitches were throbbing but she was excited to see Hank's car already at home. She raced upstairs and found the bedroom awash in candlelight. Hank had put votives everywhere—there must have been four dozen of them. Heaven could see by the flickering light that there were candles in the bathroom as well. A candlelight bubble bath maybe. Yes, the tub was full and it smelled like the pine smells of Vitabath. Only one thing was missing: Hank. Heaven found him fast asleep in bed, hidden by a pile of medical journals. She kissed his forehead and started making the rounds, blowing out candles. She even pulled the plug on the bubble bath. It lost its appeal as a lone bather activity.

"It's the thought that counts," Heaven said as she jumped into bed and drifted rapidly into sleep.

Chapter 17

Heaven looked around the kitchen of Cafe Heaven. She had just written a note to the crew and promised Brian he wouldn't have to work a double today. The judging at the contest was scheduled to be over by four in the afternoon so Heaven could be back in time to work dinner. She had looked at the total sales from last night and the reservations for tonight. It was turning into a good weekend for the restaurant. Heaven checked the time. It was six forty-five in the morning and she had fifteen minutes to get to the contest. She shot out the door before the first employee arrived and asked that first time-consuming question of the day.

The activity level at the parking lot that was now Barbeque Village was already at a minor peak when Heaven arrived. A local television station was hosting a pancake breakfast and cookers were taking paper plates stacked with pancakes back to their teammates. There were banners and Confederate flags and three-dimensional pigs flying from poles. The morning was cool and crisp but sunny. It appeared to Heaven from looking around that the most popular hangover remedy was to start drinking beer immediately upon waking up. She made her way to the Que Queens' camp, where Alice Aron was visiting from her hotel team camp, sharing pancakes and beer with Barbara and Meridith. Stephanie and Sally Jo had just arrived, Stephanie in the brightest pink cowboy boots in the two-state area.

"What shall I do first?" Heaven asked.

"Listen to all the gossip we've collected overnight and spray the ribs," Barbara directed.

The Que Queens used a popular-style meat smoker, the Tennessee Mo. The smoker was the same approximate size and shape as a fifty-gallon oil drum, if you took that oil drum and made a door in it along the long side and then put legs on it so it was parallel to the ground. On one side of the smoker was a drum about half that size, the firebox. On the other side was an upright drum, the warming box. All of these metal drums were welded together so the firebox created the heat that moved into the next chamber, the smoker, and cooked the meat. When the meat was deemed done it was transferred into the warming box, the drum farthest from the fire. Now Heaven opened the top of the middle chamber and poked at the slabs of ribs. She moved the three slabs that were on the top rack to the bottom and the four on the bottom to the top. As she moved them, she sprayed them with a plastic spray bottle filled with apple cider. Lots of cookers used apple juice to moisten their meat but Heaven liked the tang of cider better. The rest of the team let her have her way on that point.

"So, what's the gossip?" Heaven asked as she worked

Alice Aron was ready but Barbara jumped up, waving her hands. "Wait, Alice, preface, preface. Heaven, do you remember last night when you asked was there anyone in Kansas City who could win the Series? I said Pigpen had the best standing and then Pigpen's teammates yelled at us and we ran out of the party?"

"I remember every last glare and grimace," Heaven shouted from the mouth of the smoker. "So?"

"So," Alice took up the story, "the competition teams got a printout of their total points for the year last night, so everyone could see what they were up against. Of course, different parts of the country score differently, but when you see a team that consistently gets ten out of ten or nine out of nine possible points, you know they are gonna cause you some grief. Well, much to everyone's amazement, guess who was the second highest Kansas City team in total points for the year?''

"You?" everyone said more or less at the same time.

Alice shook her head. "I wish. No, it was Ben Franklin."

Everyone tittered. "Sure, Alice. Who are his teammates, George Washington and Thomas Jefferson?" Heaven cracked.

Alice pointed her pancake fork over to the far corner of the parking lot. There was a black 1955 Cadillac parked there, with all its doors open and smoke coming from the trunk area. "Over there. Ben Franklin."

"What does he do, smoke his ribs in the trunk of that big, old boat?" Heaven asked.

"Oh, no. Nothing that common. He uses woks. And he has a mute midget helper, that's his entire team, and he isn't friendly to other cookers and . . ."

Heaven closed the lid of the smoker and plopped down at a chair around the table. She grabbed a link sausage from Barbara's plate and took a nibble. "Whoa, slow down. This sounds like a great story. There's a guy who comes to the contests in an old Cadillac, smokes his meat in woks, has a mute midget for a team and he's Kansas City's front-runner, besides the deceased, God rest his soul. Is that it in a nut-shell, Alice?"

"A mute *black* midget," Alice replied, "but other than that small detail you've got a handle on it."

"Why haven't we heard about this guy before?" Heaven asked.

"Well, you don't come to that many contests, just the ones the Queens do their thing at or when you judge. When you do the Battle of the Sexes, you're busy trying to get people to throw money in the pot for the Food Bank. When you judge, you're in the judging area or with your friends. This guy would not be throwing down a few beers with Barbara's team or my team, I can assure you. But, boy, was everyone shocked when we saw how well he's done this year. Of course, everyone starts from scratch here at the Series, so it doesn't mean anything for this contest except ol' Ben is someone to beat,'' Alice said. ''Speaking of getting beat, I better get back to my campsite or those boys that work for me will have everything looking like charcoal briquettes. They want to cook everything at Warp Nine.'' Alice waved as she walked down the lane between campers and tables and tents. ''Raise lots of money,'' she yelled over her shoulder.

The next three hours passed by on fast-forward. Heaven was dying to go check out the wok guy but there was no time. She had to help the team get ready for the Battle of the Sexes before she went inside to judge. Luckily the charity teams only competed in three categories: pork, brisket and ribs. The pork shoulder and beef brisket had been on the fire since midnight and at mid-morning they were ready to go in the warming box after several dips in sauce. The Queens didn't marinate with sauce until the end, but they did put a marinade on the pork shoulder and a dry rub on the ribs and the brisket before they started the cooking process.

Pork Marinade

½ cup dark soy sauce
½ cup light soy sauce
½ cup dry sherry
½ cup rice wine vinegar
½ cup lime juice, fresh squeezed or bottled key
    lime juice
1 cup peanut oil or canola oil
¼ cup sesame oil
2 medium onions
6–10 cloves garlic
2–4 inches fresh ginger, peeled

Combine onions that have been quartered, garlic and the ginger that has been cut in several chunks in the food processor. Puree and add the oil while the processor is on. Combine these and all the other ingredients. Let rest for an hour or so before using to allow the flavors to marry. Because of all the ingredients with a sugar content—sherry and soy—this marinade imparts a deep brown color. If possible, keep your meat wrapped for part of the cooking process. Of course, if you use this for pork tenderloins or chops, the cooking time is short enough for the marinade not to burn. This marinade is great on duck, too. Just prick the skin of the duck all over, let sit in the marinade 1–2 hours and roast at 400 degrees for about 1½–2 hours or until the duck skin is crisp and loose from the meat. This means the thick layer of fat under the skin has self-basted itself away.

The grounds around the arena were slowly filling up with sightseers, young couples pushing baby buggies, families eating funnel cakes and hot dogs for breakfast and Series officials zipping around on golf carts. Cooking team members generally specialized in one part of the cooking process, one tended the fire, one made the sauce, one did the cooking of the meat. So team members were apt to wander when they weren't actually doing their job, spreading beer and information from one campsite to another. Paul Taylor appeared at the Queens' booth with both.

"Hey, Paul. Heard you were sick yesterday. Feel better?" Heaven asked as the big man walked into their territory. Stephanie rolled her eyes behind Paul's back.

"I'm okay. I just made a fool out of myself yesterday at the, you know, cemetery. I'm sorry if I hurt you yesterday when I almost fell, Heaven. My wife said if I didn't stay home last night she'd have me committed to the mental hospital." Paul laughed weakly. "I guess I was more upset about Pigpen being murdered and the pressure of getting ready for this whole thing, and, well, I guess I'm pretty disappointed I didn't make the cut. Ben Franklin, who's been cooking one year, makes it to the World Series and Paul Taylor, who's been cooking twenty years, doesn't. By the way, I didn't tear your jacket or anything yesterday when I fell on you, did I?'' Paul was staring across the heads of the women in the general direction of the Cadillac. He snapped back to earth and took a pull on his beer can. ''Heaven, I just wanted to tell you how sorry I am about everything. I heard what happened to you on your way home the other night. You should think about moving from that neighborhood. I hear those Vietnamese have gangs with blood sacrifice. And I'll be glad to send your clothes to the cleaners if you would like.''

Heaven glared at Paul. She noticed how he had side-stepped what he was looking for in the corpse's pockets. ''My jacket is just fine. Thursday was a very strange night, Paul. You crawling around at the commissary, then someone tries to run me off the road and shoots at me, now I hear that I stole Pigpen's sauce recipe that night. I wonder where that wild lie came from? Maybe from the real thief, eh, Paul?''

Paul shifted his big frame back and forth. ''I'm sure no one stole it. I'm sure the recipe will turn up in some of Pigpen's stuff.''

Stephanie couldn't resist. ''Yeah, maybe in some of his clothes.''

Paul blushed and turned around toward the path. ''I have to go. I'm on the M.C.P. team today. May the best man win.''

As he headed back to the other side of the stage where the Male Chauvinist Pig team was located, the Queens all started talking at once.

''What was that all about?''

''Poor thing, having to cook for charity like us peons instead of for the big bucks.''

''Heaven, I didn't like the way he looked at you, like you

knew something he didn't want you to. He kept staring at your jacket. Or could it be your tits?''

Heaven shrugged. ''I didn't like it either but what can I do? I thought he was going to start washing my clothes with me in them. Of course, this isn't what I wore to the funeral so what was the point? This is my week to be in the wrong place at the wrong time and I've done a great job of it if I do say so myself. Paul needs to settle down''—Heaven remembered the piece of paper she thought she saw him put in his pocket after the casket episode—''and watch out. We're going to beat the boys all the way to Topeka today. Unfortunately, I won't be here for our moment of triumph. I need to leave in a minute and go in to the judges' area. What else should I do?''

''Help us with our tiaras and sashes,'' Stephanie said. The Que Queens used their name for all it was worth. They had tacky rhinestone tiaras and pink satin sashes à la Queen Elizabeth to wear during the voting. It was a people's choice vote so they tried to give more than just a good rib to the crowd.

''No way. You're the stylist. If you can't get those damn things straight, no one can. Please don't let anyone take a picture of Barbara with her crown crooked. I see a CNN cameraman moving this way,'' Heaven said to really get Stephanie going. She had seen the camera truck pull up about an hour ago but the camera was clear across the field, over by Bo Morales and his authentic chuck wagon.

Heaven slipped in one of the side doors of the livestock exhibition building where they had met for the cooks' meeting the night before. There were pipe-and-drape curtains forming a room in the big empty building. The Charlais cows and Anaconda roosters and Suffolk sheep would be filling the building next month, when the actual American Royal would take place. Now the judges took a corner of the immense space and filled it with eight tables, each with six chairs around. About half the chairs were filled already and Heaven spotted Murray Steinblatz. She made a beeline for his table.

"Hey, babe. Sit down here. They don't allow husbands and wives to sit together but they didn't say anything about bosses and employees."

"Murray, give me a break. They didn't say anything about friends either. Boss, indeed. You make me feel like some foreman on the chain gang or something."

As the room filled up, Murray and Heaven tried to spot the celebrity judges. "We've got one of each of the major celebrity groups," Murray declared. "A Kansas City Chief . . ."

"Which one?" Heaven asked.

"How would I know? Okay, a sports figure, unknown. For a media figure, we got that lifestyle jerk on CNN, what's his name?"

"How would I know?" Heaven said with a laugh. "We really are on top of this stuff. I do know the performing arts representative, however. It's Dwight Brooks, the country singer who just signed to start a fast-food barbeque chain."

Murray piped up, "And of all things, I actually am a friend of the culinary star, Simone Springer, celebrity chef and cookbook author. We were neighbors in New York." Murray looked sad, the way he always did when he mentioned his life in New York. Heaven knew he was still damaged from his wife's death.

"Before she went off to Paris to teach the French how to cook?" Heaven's voice was laden with sarcasm.

Murray defended his old friend. "Well, you know, she teaches that California cuisine, natural, fresh, the Alice Waters thing."

"So a girl from New Jersey goes to Paris to teach them how to cook California. What a business," Heaven mused.

Just as Heaven finished her catty comments about Simone Springer, the celebrated cook appeared in the flurry of her entourage and headed for their table.

"Be nice," Murray pleaded.

"Okay, I'll do my best," Heaven said to keep Murray a little scared.

What came next showed that Murray could still schmooze with the best of them. The kiss, kiss, I've missed you so, could have been performed at Le Cirque, it was that good. Heaven gushed to make Murray happy. Simone Springer settled down at her place, her assistant by her side. Soon it was time for their final instructions and the oath.

The head barbeque judge of the World Series of Barbeque was at the microphone. "Thank you for taking the time to read the scoring guidelines in advance and a special thanks to those of you who took the judges' certification course. The categories today and their order will be: Sausage, and for this contest there are no limits as to what the sausage is made with. Each contestant must include a note card labeling their sausage as Italian, Alligator, whatever. The next category is poultry. Again, there are no limitations; it can be any poultry such as chicken or duck or turkey. The contestants have been asked to label their entries. Next will be ribs and they must be pork ribs; then pork, and at this contest, that must be shoulder, either Boston butt or arm picnic. The pork can be presented either sliced, pulled or chopped. All three of these are acceptable. After pork we will judge lamb, any cut, and, finally, beef brisket. We tried to take you from the lightest meats to the heaviest meats.

"Remember how to score. Do not compare the entries with each other. Judge each on its own merits. Try to taste and score an entry before you taste the next entry. Ten is the highest score. When the entry is placed in front of you it has a ten. You then grade down from that ten. The scoring categories are appearance, taste and tenderness. Do not talk to other judges until all of you have scored all of the entries in front of you. Do not attempt to influence the other judges at your table with facial gestures.

"You will not know whose barbeque you are tasting. Each entry has been given a new number in addition to the number on the container. Even if you saw 500 series numbers on the containers at a friend's campsite, those numbers have been changed.

"Remember the garnish rules: only leaf lettuce and curly parsley are allowed. No puddling of sauce is allowed. Sauce can be applied on the entry but no extra containers of sauce can be submitted. This includes lettuce cups.

"Please ask your team captain for bottled water when you need it. No alcohol is allowed in the judging area. We ask that any judges who have already drunk alcohol today take themselves off the judging panel. There is no smoking in the judging area and we ask that all judges refrain from smoking until the judging is completed.

"Please mark your ballots with the pencils provided. We have an old-fashioned scanning device and it's very temperamental. Try to stay in the lines when you mark your ballots. Your judge number is on the back of your chair and your table number is written on the butcher paper at one end of the table. These numbers must be on your ballots.

"Now, will everyone stand and raise their right hand. It's time to take the oath."

Heaven still got a kick out of this part of the performance, even though she had been judging contests for several years. It was proof positive that this was important business. Simone Springer was rolling her eyes and breaking the facial gesture rule already. She obviously felt taking an almost blood oath to judge a measly barbeque contest was beneath her. She raised her hand anyway.

The head judge administered the oath to the forty-eight judges and they repeated after him, "I do solemnly swear to evaluate to the best of my abilities each barbeque meat on its own merits. I accept this duty so that barbeque will survive and grow, along with truth, justice, and the American way." Heaven could hear the Superman music theme in her head. As they sat back down, the first trays of meat were headed their way.

Before the six trays of meat were set in front of them, the table captain put a paper place mat in front of each judge.

The paper mat was labeled JUDGING PLATE and each one had six squares printed on it, with Contestant Number on top of each square. The six trays of meat each had a contestant number and Heaven and the others copied those numbers onto the appropriate squares. Then the trays were opened and the judges all stood up to look up and down the table at the appearance of the six sausage entries. A couple of the tables had seven entries to take care of the fifty teams.

Heaven graded down two of the entries because they were overcrowded, slices of sausages crammed in and going every which way. She graded down one because the sausage had been left whole. How were they going to get six slices of sausage out of one huge sausage, break it off like French bread or cut it with a plastic fork? All the entries had the legal garnish of lettuce and parsley, which Heaven hated. She always wanted to see purple kale, shredded basil, edible flowers. Of course she knew this was heretic thinking. Flowers on barbeque, yuck. Heaven's own food was mercifully free of garnish, but these horrible Styrofoam containers needed something in the way of presentation. Quickly she scored the rest of the entries and nodded to the table captain that she was done. As soon as everyone was done scoring appearance, they passed out slices from each container and put them on the appropriate square on their place mats. The table captain used his pocketknife to cut the sausage that was whole. Heaven moved from top to bottom, left to right. She scored each entry for taste and tenderness, then moved on to the next. Most of the sausages were pork-based, in the country sausage or Italian sausage style. There was one delicious crayfish and rice boudin. Heaven bet it came from a Louisiana cooking team. There was also a spicy chicken and sage sausage that must have had a little cinnamon in it. When the whole table had finished, the team captain whisked the trays away and everyone started talking more or less at once.

"What about number six?"

"Too much sage in that chicken mixture."

"Did you see the smoke ring on number three?"

"Number one was drowned in sauce, you couldn't tell what the sausage was."

Simone Springer drummed her fingers on the tabletop. "Of course, after the charcuteries of France, these attempts are amusing at best."

It was going to be a long afternoon.

Two hours later, Murray and Heaven emerged from the building like moles coming out of their burrows into the sunlight. They squinted at each other.

"Your friend was sure a bucket of laughs," Heaven spit. "Now I have a stomachache from two things, barbeque and holding myself back from strangling her."

"Oh, she's just trying to show off. She's a big deal in Europe and she wants to make sure everyone here knows it," Murray said with a touch of apology in the tone of his voice.

"I'm going over to the Food Bank booth and see what happened with the Battle of the Sexes. Are you going to meet Miss La-Dee-Da?"

Murray nodded. "But of course, tea at the Ritz at four. Will you be at the cafe tonight?"

Heaven pecked Murray on the cheek. "But of course, dinner for two hundred at five. See you there."

As Heaven made her way across Barbeque Village she was distracted by a team of twelve-year-old clog dancers, then by a whole cooking team walking by in cow aprons and cow hats, black and white spots. Onstage, a country-gospel group was singing "Achy Breaky Heart" with religious words substituted for the worldly variety. The smell of hot grease wafted over from the funnel-cake wagon. It was a sight and sound and smell for sore eyes. Heaven saw someone waving at her across the way. It was Barbara Carollo, resplendent in satin sash and tiara, holding a bottle of Boulevard beer, a local brew. "We won. Heaven, we won," she yelled.

Heaven made it to the collection center for the Food Bank

and was embraced by a tipsy Barbara. "We got twice as many votes as they did. Their ribs weren't cooked enough. They were tough as shoe leather, you could barely gnaw them off the bone," she giggled. "Paul was off his stride and the other guys too. Maybe they don't hate women enough to have the killer instinct ol' Pigpen did."

Heaven checked her watch. "Barbara, I'm thrilled. How much money did we make and what can I do to help break down?"

Barbara held up two fingers. "Twelve hundred big ones and all that food," she said as she waved her hands loosely in the direction of the trash containers full of canned goods. "Two of the guys that work for me came down and they have the camp almost put away. Stephanie is supervising. I know you have to go cook, so get."

"What about you?" Heaven asked. "It is the busiest night of the week in the restaurant business and you are a chef."

"Yes, but I have a sous chef and you don't. I'll sober up and go in about six. Now go. I'll see you tomorrow at the bash at your place. Do you need help for tomorrow, by the way?"

"I'll call if I get panicky. Thanks for letting me off the hook on cleanup."

Barbara turned to walk away and then paused. "Oh, yeah. How was the best barbeque in the world?"

"Good sausage, great ribs, tough brisket." Heaven waved and turned toward the car. But she wasn't quite ready to leave the world of barbeque. She knew she didn't have time for both, so she took a quarter out of her jean jacket pocket and tossed it in the air. "Heads, it's Bo Morales, tails the wok guy." The quarter flipped through the air and landed tails. Heaven picked up the coin off the ground. "It's just as well," she sighed and headed off toward the Cadillac in the corner of the parking lot, just under the highway overpass that led suburban families down to the Bottoms from their homes out south. It wasn't exactly the choice spot.

Heaven had an idea from what she had heard about this Ben Franklin guy that he had probably alienated someone on the site committee and had been banished to the Kansas City equivalent of Siberia. But there were plenty of hangers-on over here too. It looked like Ben was popular with the crowd. Soon Heaven could understand why there were sightseers.

Ben Franklin had on a wild outfit that included a silk top hat that had seen better days but was completely covered with barbeque contest buttons, denim overalls but no shirt underneath, six tattoos that Heaven could see and red high-top sneakers with feathers glued all over them. He was carrying an open umbrella that was big enough to fit over a golf cart or outdoor cafe table. "Here," he was saying as he held out a tray of samples, "taste these ribs and tell me you tasted better. You can't, cause there are no better, right, Mickey?"

The black midget assistant nodded yes silently.

Heaven couldn't stand it. Mickey, the mute midget. This made the surreal aspects of the funeral yesterday almost pale by comparison. Heaven walked around to the back of the car while Ben was entertaining in front. She glanced in the vintage Caddie and saw a sleeping bag in the back seat, along with lots of tongs, spatulas, foil and dirty kitchen towels. One-stop shopping. Heaven was afraid she was too late to see Ben's rig. Lots of teams had packed up for the day. But she was in luck. There it stood, a Rube Goldberg-esque tower of giant woks, the kind they used in those huge Chinatown restaurants in San Francisco. Some of them were facing wide mouth to wide mouth and formed giant metal clams. Some of them had holes drilled in them, presumably to allow the heat to reach the smoking chamber. Some of them were rowed up side by side to form a caterpillar-like middle to the contraption. Heaven bet that's where the meat went. She made a note to visit Ben Franklin next weekend when she was scheduled to do night duty at the Queens' camp. She wanted to see the thing in action.

Suddenly she felt the presence of someone near. Mickey was standing near her elbow staring at her staring at the wok/smoker.

"This is really great. I hear you've won a lot this year with this rig. How do you break it down?" Heaven immediately realized small talk was impossible, however appropriate, with Mickey. But he was mute, not deaf. He walked over to the middle section of the device and pointed to a joint that was fitted with washers and nuts and bolts. A piece of chimney flue was leading to the next wok. Heaven could now see that the smoker broke down into three big pieces that would fit on the tiny flatbed trailer that was connected to the Cadillac. Heaven nodded. "I see. Thanks," she said. Mickey pointed to her judge's badge. "Oh, yes. I did judge today," Heaven said as she removed her badge hurriedly. Heaven usually took off her badge before she started walking around. Even though everyone knew the judging was blind, sometimes cookers started describing the sheen of the glaze over their brisket and they expected Heaven to remember and tell them they had received a perfect score. Of course, this would not happen with Mickey.

But Mickey did the equivalent. He grabbed Heaven by the arm and pulled her around toward Ben Franklin. He was now pointing to the pocket of her jean jacket where she had stashed the judge's badge. As tempted as she was, Heaven just didn't have time to meet another character. She shook her head at Mickey and shook his hand and made a little bow. With that she made a beeline for the parking lot. It was, after all, Saturday night and she had her own cooking to do.

Chapter 18

She knew it was time. Heaven cursed herself for saying yes. *Just what I need,* she thought. *After the busiest Saturday in months, I have to haul my ass out of bed and go make a party. I've ruined the only day off together Hank and I have. I've ruined the only day I have off, period.* She refused to open her eyes and ducked under the quilts again and felt around for Hank. No one was there. *Well, I guess I might as well get up too. No snuggling today.* Heaven's feet touched the floor just as the phone rang. It was nine o'clock on Sunday morning.

"Rise and shine, H. It's your personal news service." It was Stephanie.

Heaven smiled in spite of her ardent desire to be crabby. "Okay, let me have it, baby. You do know I had to go to work and I don't have a clue who came out on top of yesterday's round. I hope you . . ."

Stephanie interrupted. "Of course. I even tried to call you last night but Mr. Steinblatz said you couldn't possibly talk."

"Good for Mr. Steinblatz. We were swamped. We did almost three hundred. So?"

"So it's just as we figured. Bo Morales is in fourth place, out of the serious money, but that can change. Number three is the lovely Felicity June Morgan. Number two in the standings goes to Eleazar Martin, king of Memphis."

"Does that mean that Pigpen's team came through, that they made first place?"

"No way. Alice Aron's team placed above those sad-eyed boys. Alice was seventh. No, guess again."

Heaven spotted a note on the mirror from Hank and she padded over to it with the cordless phone. WENT TO MOM'S, CHURCH, LUNCH WITH HER. LOVE, HANK. Heaven pulled it down and kissed it before she tossed it in the trash basket. "The team from Seattle?"

"Heaven, this is much more fun than a bunch of salmon smokers. Who did we talk about, just yesterday morning?"

"Oh, no, not Ben Franklin. I went over and checked him out before I left. It can't be Ben and Mickey. Can't you see them accepting a trophy and the check? What a sight for CNN."

"Oh, they're already on CNN. I saw it last night. They did a good three minutes of Ben showing how that wok rig works. What a fashion statement he is."

"Stephanie, this is big news. This will make the party very interesting. Do you think that Ben Franklin was even invited to this thing?"

"No way. The only people invited to this 'do' were supposed to be the judges and the out-of-town teams. Of course, Kansas City Barbeque Guild people and the World Series Committee are included, and you asked your teammates. This is the last social event until next Friday. Most of the judges and some of the teams will fly home during the week and come back next weekend. The city gave them permission to leave their smokers down in the parking lot and the committee hired security guards. But, hell, you're the one having this soiree. Don't you know what the deal is?"

Heaven shook her head at the phone. "All I know is the head count is one hundred eighty, that's all I wanted to know. Will you come over early and help primp the serving area? I think we'll put the food back by the stage. That way, beer and champagne at the bar, food at the back, make people circulate."

"Why not put the food on the stage?" Stephanie asked, always wanting to make a visual splash.

"Because we're having a samba band on the stage."

"Thank God. If you'd told me we were having the clog dancers or that horrible country singer I'd have developed a sick headache."

"By that horrible country singer I assume you mean Dwight Brooks. I think he's one of our guests tonight. Now I have to get off the phone and start on this."

"What time do you want me?" Stephanie asked.

"This is a cocktail party, six to eight, so could you come over about four?"

"See you then."

An hour later, when Heaven turned on the lights in the cafe kitchen, she finally saw the potential of the evening. This could be very interesting and maybe even fun. Now, what to do first?

Heaven realized lots of team members hadn't had much time to eat out in Kansas City, so she knew part of the menu had to be barbeque. She also knew that the judges were probably all as sick of barbeque as she was today so she had tried to devise a menu that would satisfy both groups. Heaven had asked the woman in her neighborhood who owned a popular Viet restaurant to make summer rolls, the unfried version of spring rolls that was a Vietnamese specialty. The rice-paper skins were filled with cilantro, shrimp, pork and soft rice noodles, then rolled like a cigar and served with a spicy dipping sauce.

Viet Summer Rolls

2 carrots, peeled and shredded
Bean sprouts, mung bean sprouts or other sprouts such as sunflower seed or mustard
1 pkg. rice-stick noodles, soaked in warm water for 30 minutes
Leaf lettuce

Cilantro leaves and mint leaves
1 pork tenderloin, marinated in the pork marinade
   and roasted 20 minutes at 350 degrees.
½ lb. large shrimp, boiled and peeled
1 pkg. rice-paper wrappers.

Soak carrots in 1 T. sugar for 20 minutes. In a large pot, boil water and blanch the pre-soaked noodles for a minute, then rinse them in cold water. Mix the carrots and cilantro and mint leaves in with the noodles and coarsely chop the mix so the noodles will fit in the roll better. Slice pork thinly and slice shrimp lengthwise. Fill a bowl with warm water. Take the rice-paper wrappers one at a time and dunk them in the warm water. Lay them carefully on a paper towel and begin to build your rolls. Put a leaf of lettuce down on top of the wrapper, add a spoonful of the noodle mixture and spread it the long way. Put three slices of pork on top of the noodles, fold the sides of the wrapper inward and start rolling. After a couple of rolls, place shrimp slices and bean sprouts on the wrapper and finish wrapping. Use a damp paper towel to protect the finished rolls until serving. I sometimes chop up peanuts, basil leaves or shred a cucumber to add to the noodle mix.

Ginger Dipping Sauce

2–4 garlic cloves, crushed and diced
2 T. sugar
1 fresh chili, such as jalapeno
2 T. grated fresh ginger
2 T. toasted sesame seeds
¼ cup each of lime juice and Nuoc Mam (fish
   sauce)

Split and deseed the chili and dice. Combine all ingredients and let sit at least 30 minutes before using.

One of the night crew had come in early yesterday to construct some California rolls. They were rolled up in their seaweed, on trays in the walk-in, ready to be cut into portions. Heaven would save that job for Sara, who was coming in at two to help. Heaven knew no one else wanted to work seven days a week, but Sara had volunteered, saying she didn't mind if she could leave by eight.

Heaven put on a big pot of water to boil. She was going to make one of her well-known dishes, cold soy noodles with a ginger soy sauce. She had ordered a case of fresh Chinese egg noodles from the Chinese grocery store. They only took seconds to cook, and she'd make the dressing while the water came to a boil.

Next on Heaven's prep list was the word "wings." She wasn't planning to serve this group a mundane version of buffalo wings. She was keeping with her oriental theme and planned caramelized Viet chicken wings, a dish made by braising the wings in caramelized sugar and fish sauce. She knew she needed to get them on soon, before anyone else arrived. The smell of fish sauce was not popular with the Cafe Heaven crew but they loved the finished product. These wings had been on the menu as a starter last spring.

Viet Chicken Wings

2 lbs. chicken wings
caramel sauce, cooled (see following recipe)
2–4 inches ginger, peeled and sliced
6 cloves garlic, peeled and sliced
2 stalks lemongrass, sliced
2 kifer lime leaves
4 shallots, thinly sliced

Combine all ingredients in a heavy saute pan, frying pan, or Dutch oven. Bring mixture to a boil, simmer 30–40 minutes or until chicken is tender. Every ten minutes or so, stir the mixture over the wings to coat.

Caramel Sauce

⅓ cup sugar
¼ cup Nuoc Mam (fish sauce)

Melt sugar in a heavy saucepan, stirring constantly. When it is brown, remove from heat and stir in fish sauce. The mixture will bubble up. Put back on heat until the sugar is completely dissolved, about 3–5 minutes. Cool thoroughly. Always use cold sauce and bring it up to temperature along with the chicken wings or the sauce will turn to globs of sugar.

Wontons were next on the list and Heaven peeked in the freezer to see if they had already been assembled. They were there, filled with a wasabi, pickled ginger, and mascarpone cheese mixture and twisted into little bags, ready to be fried. Yes, the crew came through with doing the prep work, Heaven thought, as she closed the freezer.

To allow the visiting firemen to taste the local fare, Heaven had ordered the same dish, ribs, from eight different barbecue joints around town and she had asked them to include plenty of their signature sauce with the meat. She was adding her own rib dish, grilled lamb ribs with a Thai marinade and a peanut dipping sauce. Her plan was to fill one end of the table with all the different ribs and sauces and the other end of the table with the oriental dishes. She would ask Chris to make cards labeling everything so the experts could sample their hearts out. It was a picture in her mind already. Now she had to make it so.

Thai Peanut Sauce

1 bottle Thai sweet chili sauce
roasted peanuts—dry roasted are fine
2 T. sesame oil
warm water

Empty the chili sauce into the bowl of the food processor, turn on and add peanuts. When the mixture resembles a loose peanut butter, add the sesame oil and the warm water to the consistency you want. The sauce is better stiff if you are using it as a dip for raw vegetables and with more water added for sauce with meats.

When Heaven heard the sounds of Carmen McRae in the dining room, she knew the afternoon had flown by. One of the wait staff must be there getting the dining room ready. "Sara, how long have you been here?"

Sara grinned. "Two hours and I came at two, so that makes it four and yes, my watch confirms it. Where's your watch, H?"

"It's somewhere in this kitchen. I had to take it off to mix the dressing on the noodles. I better check on the kids. Are we okay?"

Sara looked up from slicing the California rolls. "I'm almost done with this, then I'll crisp those wontons, then grill the ribs and we're done. You did the wings and noodles and marinated the ribs and made sauces. The rest is a piece a cake."

Heaven went out the swinging door of the kitchen into the dining room just as Stephanie Simpson came in the front door, her hands full of props. Sam rushed over to help her. "What is all this stuff?" he asked.

Stephanie put down a sack that was labeled RIVER ROCKS on the outside. "Whoa, these are heavy. Sam, there are some palm fronds out in the car, would you go get them, sweetie? Please and thank you. The answer to your question is this is atmosphere, darling, decor, ambiance. I will work magic, as usual.''

Heaven hugged her friend. "You just happen to have palm fronds and river rocks around the house. That's what I love about you. I just happen to have some white sand if you want to do the Zen garden thing. It's downstairs on some shelf. Have Sam get it if you need it. All I ask is that this be a sophisticated cocktail-party table, not a funky bar-beque table. We can't beat them at their game, so we'll play a different one.''

"Of course," Stephanie said as she started pulling tables together. "We'll transport them for a couple of hours, samba music, Vietnamese food, exotic locale, danger, intrigue. I can see it now.''

And by five-thirty, so could everyone else.

Chapter 19

Simone Springer leaned back in the booth and twirled her toothpick with the olive stuck on it. "There's just nothing like a Bombay martini for lunch, now is there, Paul?"

"I wouldn't know. I've never tasted a martini in my life. I'm a beer man, Ms. Springer," Paul Taylor said as he squirmed uncomfortably. Paul had only water in front of him.

"Simone. Call me Simone, Paul. After all, we're buddies now. You could say we're even business partners."

"Simone, I think you have the wrong idea here. You're way off base. But even if you, well, I just don't understand what I can ever do for you. What do you want? Aside from making Dwight Brooks mad, of course."

Simone drank the last of her martini and signaled the waiter for another. The Ritz-Carlton lounge was almost empty. It was still church time on Sunday, for God's sake. No one decent swilled martinis this early on Sunday.

"Oh, Paul, I think I'm right about this one. I have a gut feeling that I've caught you being very bad, now haven't I? When I called you last week and told you I would double any money Mr. Brooks offered for any sauce or marinade or whatever, you were very helpful. And when I talked to your friend Pigpen, he got quite a chuckle out of my little plan to cost Dwight money. Said he'd already heard from Dwight and he guessed he'd just have to call the poor boy back and tell him how the price went up. I asked Mr. Hopkins why you recomended him to both Dwight and myself. He said it was because he made the best sauce in Kansas City. Then he laughed a rather frightening laugh and said you knew what side your bread was buttered on. That Pigpen really had a way with words.''

Paul Taylor tried putting on a brave front but it failed. ''So?'' he said too loudly. The bartender and waiter looked up from the wine cooler they were stocking.

''So it's hard for me to believe you didn't have something to do with Pigpen's untimely demise in the sauce. You knew more than anyone about his double-dealing, didn't you, Paul? What double deal was he running on you that made you kill him?''

Paul Taylor shook his head. ''I didn't kill him. I think I'll take you up on that beer, though.'' He raised his hand to get the waiter's attention. So you think I'm responsible for Pigpen? Then why not go to the police and tell them your theory? Why come to me?''

Simone leaned across the table and patted Paul's big hand. ''So you can help me with my little revenge, Paul. Where is the famous Pigpen sauce recipe? I know you know.''

The place looked great. Stephanie had created a kind of colonial empire look, with some Indian sari silk draped over parts of the table. She spread the palms over the rest of the table except for a circle that was off center toward the middle. She filled the circle with white sand and combed it into a wavy pattern. Three black rocks made a Zen non-pattern on the sand. She'd even sent Sam to her house for a Krishna bronze sculpture and an old wicker suitcase. The sculpture was placed off center in the sand and the open suitcase was lined with a tablecloth and held crocks with all the different sauces. There were big white platters for the ribs and patterned oriental platters for the wings and noodles. A rattan tray held the filled wontons and California rolls. Heaven had three Japanese tea bowls and Stephanie had put the wasabi, pickled ginger, and soy sauce in those. Chris had picked up all the different ribs and now was busy making the labels. He and Sam were there to keep the tables filled and pour champagne. One of the bartenders was also there to pull beers. Murray had come in to meet and greet and the samba band was softly tuning up onstage. Heaven paced around one last time, checking the lights, sticking her head into the kitchen to make sure Sara didn't need her and counting the bottles of champagne.

Murray shook his head. "Ya know, boss, if you don't have to be in the kitchen tonight, why don't you take off that chef's coat and apron?"

Heaven looked down at her apron. It had ginger and soy dressing all over it. "Oh, shit. I brought cute clothes to change into. They're still in the van. Thanks for the gentle reminder, Murray. I'll be right back."

When Heaven reappeared in a short black dress and her new Italian high-heeled boots, the room was filling up fast. Most of the cooking teams were already there, having to uphold their reputation for being able to drink more at a two-hour cocktail party than most groups do in four. She noticed all the front-runners except Ben Franklin. Murray was busy introducing Simone Springer around. Bo Morales was deep in conversation with Felicity Morgan. Heaven saw Paul Taylor come in the door and look around uneasily. When he saw Heaven, he started across the floor toward her. I'm not in the mood, Heaven thought, and turned her back on that part of the room. I better find someone to talk to, fast. An oversized cowboy hat came into Heaven's field of vision. Perfect. Heaven moved quickly toward Dwight Brooks.

"Mr. Brooks, I'm Heaven Lee. Welcome to my cafe. I hear you're going in the restaurant business yourself soon."

Dwight Brooks swept his hat off with a flourish. "Heaven, you may call me crazy, but a man has to make hay while the sun shines. Now, while I've got a little extra cash, I figure I better plan for the future, have my money working for me while I'm out there on that tour bus. And darlin', call me Dwight.''

"Yes, well, Dwight, barbeque is very popular now but it's such a personal thing. How do you think it will translate to a chain?''

"Heaven, you are sure insightful, yes sir. Of course it's personal. Everyone thinks the barbeque from their part of the country is the best. But we can make that work for us, Heaven. Yes sir—I mean ma'am.''

Heaven hated being called ma'am but she could see Paul Taylor looking over the head of Felicity Morgan in her direction. She wouldn't drop her cover for one little ma'am infraction. She grabbed Dwight Brooks's elbow and steered him toward the food table. "So what's your plan, Dwight? And please don't call me ma'am. It makes me feel like an old lady.''

"And I certainly did not mean to imply that,'' Dwight said with something like a leer on his face. He grabbed a plate and started piling on ribs, one from each barbeque joint. "Why, you must have done this for me, Heaven. A whole smorgasboard of Kansas City barbeque, all in one place. Now back to my plan. Dwight Brooks Smokin' Que will have the best of the whole country: Kansas City, Texas, Memphis, South Carolina. We'll have sauces from all those cities, the top of the towns, right at the Smokin' Que. So no matter if you're in Boise or Des Moines, if you like Texas-style brisket it'll be there. If you want South Carolina pulled pork, we'll have it.''

Heaven picked up a small plate and started spooning on a taste of all nine barbecue sauces, including her own Thai peanut sauce. "Well, then, you have died and gone to Heaven, so to speak. Here is a comparison taste test of all the best in Kansas City. Knock yourself out.''

Murray and Simone Springer walked up to the food table and Simone actually acted interested. Paul Taylor appeared too, lurking around the California rolls. Heaven turned toward Simone, the lesser of two evils right now. "Heaven, darling, what a clever idea. What do we have here? A pu-pu platter of sorts? Murray, please fix me a plate, darling, but Heaven, we don't have anything with peanuts, do we? I'm deathly allergic to them. They make my throat close up."

Heaven did her best Betty Furness hand gesture, showing Simone the labels. She grabbed another small plate and started spooning the sauces on it, then handed it to Murray. She pointed to the name tags on the food. "As *we* can see, *we* have a spicy peanut dip over here on the barbeque side that you won't even have a whiff of. Murray, be sure she gets to taste the other sauces that have made Kansas City famous, like the Arthur Bryant's. By the way, Simone, have you met Dwight Brooks? Since you live in France most of the time you might not know who Dwight is . . ."

Simone wouldn't let Heaven tell her about Dwight's Country Music Association awards. "I certainly do know, Heaven. Even in France, Mr. Brooks has a reputation. It's been a while, Dwight." The frost in the air between the two of them gave Heaven a chill. Goose bumps jumped up on her arms.

Dwight Brooks tipped his hat again with that giant gesture. He was beginning to irritate Heaven. He obviously irritated Simone, and that seemed to give him pleasure. "Simone and I have known each other for years, before she was a big culinary star and I achieved my own modest success. Simone, honey, did you know I'm gettin' in the food business myself?"

Simone was busy ignoring Dwight and dipping a rib in her sauce puddles. He launched into the fascinating story of his new fast-food chain anyway. Heaven squeezed Murray's arm and turned to check out the rest of the room.

Stephanie came sprinting her way. "You'll never guess who just came in the door," she sputtered.

As Heaven turned toward the door, she saw Jumpin' Jack enter. Jack was not invited, of course, but Heaven would not think of asking him to leave. His camo outfit turned a few heads but Heaven knew that was not who Stephanie was talking about.

Heaven could see the real object of interest. It was the man with the most points, the man who had only been cooking a year, the man to beat next weekend, Ben Franklin. He had obviously put on his Sunday go-to-meetin' clothes: a striped dress shirt, wide flowered tie and plaid sports jacket. It made the overalls of yesterday seem conservative.

"I thought he wasn't invited," Heaven asked under her breath.

Stephanie looked over at Paul Taylor, who was waving a greeting at Ben from the food table. "Well, that was before he popped up in first place. No one could ask him to leave now, could they? Ol' Paul is acting positively happy to see him. What a difference a day makes, huh, H?"

Heaven and Stephanie watched as, one by one, Bo Morales, Felicity Morgan and Eleazar Martin made their way over to shake hands with Ben Franklin. "I say we go for it. We can kill four birds with one hello," Heaven said.

"I'll go with you but don't think I haven't already spent a little time flirting with Bo baby. I nabbed him as soon as he set foot in the door," Stephanie archly confessed.

"You're a happily married woman," Heaven said sternly.

"Yes, I am, but that has nothing to do with flirting. I want to keep in practice."

"Well, come here and practice on me," a voice said. It was Felicity June Morgan who Stephanie had unknowingly walked up next to. She linked her arm with Stephanie's arm, and, with her other hand, tapped Stephanie on the nose. "You are as cute as a bug, aren't you?"

Heaven poked Stephanie in the ribs and whispered, "Serves you right," in her ear before going over to stand between Bo and Eleazar. They were listening to Ben tell the fascinating tale of how he first devised the tower of woks.

"I used to cook in a hotel with this old boy, a gook from Thailand or somewhere," Ben explained. "Well, he used to take those big ol' woks and tea smoke in them. It was the damnedest thing. Throw all this tea and rice and brown sugar down there and put his ducks, he usually did ducks, up a-ways in the wok on a rack. Then he fired that thing up and put the top on it and the thing would stink like hell but the ducks were just beautiful. It come to me in a dream last year. If that gook could smoke in one wok, why couldn't I rig 'em together and do some real smokin'?''

The three out-of-towners stared at Ben in amazement. Bo, being the slickest of the three, managed a weak smile. ''You certainly took an idea and ran with it,'' he said. ''What kind of sauce do you use?''

''Oh, now,'' Ben said with a wink. ''That's a secret between me and Mickey.''

Heaven jumped in. ''Where is Mickey tonight?'

Ben shook his head. ''He don't like parties. People put their elbows in his eyes when he stands at the buffet tables. Stomp on him. But not me, I'm goin' back there and chow down.''

Again, Ben had brought the conversation to a screeching halt. They all watched in silence as he made a beeline for the food. Heaven tried a new tactic. ''I want to congratulate all of you. I had to leave yesterday before the standings were announced. Are you all sticking around this week or going back home?''

Aza answered first. ''I'm outta here in the morning. I've got five joints to run so I'll see y'all next week. Heaven, speaking of joints, you've got a real nice place here. I think I'll go get something to eat. I hear we have some oriental food. I love Thai.''

''Then please try my lamb ribs. And be sure to use the spicy peanut sauce with them,'' Heaven offered.

Felicity was still attached to Stephanie, who was making faces at Heaven frantically. ''I'm not goin' home either and now I think I want to sample some of those good Kansas City ribs. Stephanie, sugar, will you show me the food?''

Heaven had no intention of rescuing Stephanie but she

would remind Felicity she was not a single woman. "Where is your tall friend, Felicity?"

Felicity's eyes narrowed. "Why, Heaven, darlin', she's workin' so I don't have to. Come on, sugar." Felicity led her victim away through the crowd. Stephanie looked over her shoulder at Heaven, pleading with her eyes.

Bo Morales laughed and wagged his finger at Heaven. "You better watch out, Heaven. Felicity will steal your friend."

"I'll check her pockets at the door. Bo, what about you? Will you go home this week?"

"No, not with the animals. One of the guild members has a farm and I hauled the team out there this morning. I'll stay here, tend to the mules and practice a little. After all, I'm number four. I may need your help this week," Bo said with a cute little wink. He reached out and touched her stitches but he didn't say anything about them. Who knew which version he'd heard.

Heaven could feel a blush starting. "I can't imagine you needing help with anything, Bo, but of course, I'll be glad to. . . ."

Bo laughed. "Order some meat for me wholesale, Heaven. And perhaps taste when I cook and give me a critique."

Heaven was relieved. She had been thinking the worst about Bo's intentions. Or was it her own intentions she wasn't so sure about? "Of course. Why don't we eat something? Tonight you can give me a critique on my lamb ribs."

As Heaven and Bo headed to the back of the dining room, Paul Taylor came barreling their way. "Have you seen Dwight Brooks, Heaven? I really need to see him," Paul said with worry in his voice.

"He was back by you at the buffet table with Simone," Heaven answered dryly. As they all three moved in that direction, a yell came from the guitar player onstage. Someone had knocked over the conga drum set that had been part of the percussionist's kit. Ben and Dwight and Murray and Aza and Felicity and Stephanie were hovering around a prone figure who had fallen onto the stage and was now wedged between a conga drum and its metal stand. A tambourine that had been hooked on the side of the stand was perched on the head of the fallen figure.

Jumpin' Jack pushed through the crowd and got to the body before Heaven. He initiated emergency mouth-to-mouth resuscitation and as he took a breath Heaven could see who was down. It was Simone Springer.

"Watch out, it's the Viet Cong," Jack yelled as he spotted Heaven and pulled her down on top of Simone. "They'll be back. Play dead," Jack instructed as he did an atomic bomb duck and cover over the two women. Heaven remained calm for a minute because she had seen Jack have these episodes before. Then she realized that the woman underneath her wasn't breathing. Simone Springer seemed to be dead.

Chapter 20

Detective Bonnie Weber got up to stretch and decided to take her shoes off. After all, she felt right at home at Cafe Heaven, considering how much time as she'd spent here this year. She had arrived back in town from her retreat about three. Just enough time to get comfortable with her husband and kids, get a load of laundry going. And then this.

"Katy, more coffee, please," she yelled, calling Heaven by her birth name again. Instead of Heaven, Sam ran over with the pot and poured. "Haven't you gone home yet, Sam?" Bonnie had worked her way through the cooking teams and judges and Murray and Chris and Sam. She had sent Jumpin' Jack home, even though she had doubts about his ability to roam free. She had asked Sara all about the food and the samba band all about what had been happening before the crash. She had talked to the bartender, the dishwasher, the evidence technicians and the Que Queens. She was almost talked out. "You might as well come over here, Katy, and then we are going home."

Heaven appeared with a full champagne glass in her hand and a desperate look in her eye. "Sam, Bonnie's right. Why don't you go home, honey. Everything is put back where it belongs. We can't do any more tonight. But tomorrow, Sam . . ."

Sam looked a little scared too. "We meet at Sal's?"

Heaven nodded. "You got it. Will you make the phone

calls and let me know what time you decide on?"

Sam took off and Heaven plopped down across a four-top table from Bonnie. "What did the coroner say?"

Bonnie lit a cigarette. "The coroner said it looked to him like anaphylactic shock, a severe allergic reaction. She had severe angio edema, her face was totally swollen and her throat had swollen almost closed."

"Did you tell him that she told me she was allergic to peanuts and I showed her the sauce with the peanuts in it? There was also a sign on it, for God's sake. I can't believe she would have eaten it, knowing what it would do to her. It must be something else."

Bonnie nodded. "I told the doc all that and he said thanks for the clue and I sent him a sample of the peanut sauce with the evidence techs. Heaven, word on the street has you making a plate of all the different sauces for the deceased."

"Yeah, I started a plate, then I gave it to Murray to finish."

"Did Murray hear Simone tell you she was allergic to peanuts? Maybe he didn't hear you and put some of that sauce on her plate," Bonnie asked hopefully.

"He was right there. I'm sure he heard. I'm sure everyone heard. She was very emphatic."

Murray had accompanied Simone to the hospital. The ambulance team thought the ER team might be able to revive her but it was just too late. Bonnie would have to talk to Murray tomorrow.

"Here's what we've got," Bonnie said as she held up all her legal pads. "We've got two barbeque-contest-related people murdered in a week. This is either the worst coincidence or we've got some huge plot going on. In other words, I don't know yet if they are related or just two separate cases. Or it could be that the Simone thing is not homicide at all, but a tragic accident. There are all kinds of possibilities."

"Just remember," Heaven said, "everyone ate out of the

same bowls. If there was poison in the food, everyone would have the same chance of being poisoned."

"Not if it was perfectly normal food that most people can eat easily, something that would only affect the intended victim, who had allergies," Bonnie pointed out.

"I guess that means premeditation. A person would have to know that Simone was allergic to something, in this case, peanuts, and hide it in something they knew she would eat. And not only that, it would have to be something she liked so she would eat enough to . . ." Heaven's voice trailed off.

Bonnie nodded her head. "I'm glad to see your training in criminal law hasn't failed you through lack of practice, Katy. This thing has as many turns and twists as a roller coaster. The only two people in the crowd who admit knowing Simone before this weekend are Murray and Dwight Brooks. Of course neither of them confessed and said they have always hated her for breaking their heart back in '73."

Heaven took a long drink from her sparkling wine, Gloria Ferrar. She put the glass down and promptly got up and went to the bar for the rest of the bottle. Pouring herself another, she was ready to theorize. "Here's what I hope. I hope that Pigpen was killed accidentally by a burglar who was pissed off that there wasn't anything but barbeque sauce in that kitchen. Maybe he didn't even know that Pigpen fell into the soup. And then I hope Simone just was talking and forgot what she was doing and dipped her rib into the wrong crock."

Bonnie started putting her legal pads away, a sure sign that she was done for the night. "And how do you explain away the attempt to run you off the road and shoot at you?"

Heaven's hand went up to her temple and the stitches. "As impossible as it sounds, it could have been a drive-by. Purely chance. There's one more thing that I have to know tonight. You're not going to shut me down or anything like that are you?"

Bonnie got up and stuffed her swollen feet back in her size eleven pumps. "This isn't like last time, H. Let's see what the doc says, but I don't see that the public is at risk like it was when someone was putting rhubarb leaves in the salad greens. But you, you're the only person left alive out of three murder attempts this week.''

''A thought that I've had myself. If this is a barbeque contest mystery, why me and why Simone? We're certainly on the perimeter of that world. But just to be safe, will you stay a minute so we can walk out together?''

Heaven hurried around and checked the ovens and stoves, made sure the back door was locked, set the alarm and then she and Bonnie went out the front.

Heaven crossed her fingers and hurried to Fifth Street with no incident. Hank had to work all night at the hospital so Heaven was expecting an empty house. What she wasn't expecting was how scared she would feel. It was almost one in the morning, a perfect time to call England. She could catch her daughter before she left for school. She needed to talk to Iris. And as soon as her daughter heard her voice, trying to sound normal, she knew something was up.

''Mom, what's the matter? Tell me everything.''

Heaven started to talk, then she started to cry.

Chapter 21

"This time will be harder. There are more out-of-town people involved so there are more things that will be difficult for us to learn. But we're a great team and I know we can help solve this if we pool our resources."

Heaven was giving a pep talk to her troops, who were at their investigation headquarters: Sal's barbershop. Joe, Chris and Sam were there plus Murray and Sara, all representing the cafe. Stephanie and Barbara were there from the Que Queens. Sal was there and Mona was going to try to come but customers kept coming in the cat shop. She waved wistfully at them from her shop window.

"The other thing about this case is technically we're not in as much hot water as before; this isn't a life-and-death, they'll-close-the-cafe thing. At least I don't think it is."

Chris Snyder stood up. "But it can't be good for another person to die in the cafe. I think we should try to solve this as fast as possible or people could get scared and stop liking us."

Sal nodded. "The kid's gotta point. Plus the bigger picture is you're gonna make national news cause of this Simone bein' a celebrity chef, right, Heaven?"

This was why Sal was brilliant. He could think of things to worry about that you hadn't even thought of yet. A picture of the *Hard Copy* film crew descending on Thirty-ninth Street passed through Heaven's mind. She didn't have time for that now. "Let me try to enumerate the disasters for us. Last Tuesday, Pigpen Hopkins was found dead by yours truly and Stephanie. On Thursday, we found out that Pigpen's famous sauce recipe was missing and his teammates say they don't have it. Again on Thursday I'm at the wrong place. I find Paul Taylor crawling around, supposedly looking for the recipe, then someone shoots into my car as I'm heading home. On Friday, we have Pigpen's funeral; the World Series begins. Saturday, a dark horse named Ben Franklin pulls ahead in the standings for the first weekend. On Sunday, one of the barbeque judges dies while attending a cocktail party at Cafe Heaven. She also happens to be a well-known chef and cookbook author, not just some unknown off the street. What do all these events have in common?"

You could almost see the old reporter genes in Murray kick in. He raised his hand proudly. "Broadest thing they have in common is food. Pigpen died in his sauce. Simone died from allergic food shock, we think. You were out at the commissary bottling dry rub when you were attacked on the way home."

Sal grinned, a facial gesture that was rendered bizarre because of the ever-present cigar. "So what's the point? Some idiot who doesn't like food is terrorizing the city?"

Murray was intent on his brainstorming and didn't recognize the sarcasm in Sal's crack. "Good point, Sal. It could be someone who is trying to discredit the city, a city employee with a grudge. It could be a disgruntled barbeque contest failure. And that brings us to the next thing that all the events have in common, the World Series of Barbeque. If not for the Series, Pigpen wouldn't have been making sauce and neither would the Queens. Heaven wouldn't have been bottling dry rub on Thursday. Simone wouldn't have been in Kansas City and there wouldn't have been a party at Cafe Heaven on Sunday night. What else?"

This time it was Stephanie Simpson who raised her hand.

"Oh, that's easy. The other thing all the events have in common is Heaven."

"I know you're correct about that but let's try the other doors first before we settle on me as the cause of all this. And us finding the body was such a chance encounter. No one could have planned to kill Pigpen just to scare the daylights out of me," Heaven argued.

Stephanie was not convinced. "H, I told you that the secretary at the Barbeque Guild schedules the time at the kitchen. She knew Pigpen was going to be there and also that we were going to be there. It wasn't a state secret, for God's sake. If someone asked her, she probably told them."

"Then how about you going out to Raytown to the guild headquarters and checking out the secretary to see if she had any calls about the commissary. And while you're at it, you might ask her about how they pick the judges. Why was Simone here?"

"Well, I have no one to blame but myself. I opened my mouth and now I guess I have to go to Raytown. First, I'll have to change my outfit into something more pastel," Stephanie said as she looked at her all-black Donna Karan ensemble. Raytown was not known for its sleek sophistication.

Heaven went on with her assignments. "Now, Sam, will you make one of your famous diagrams of the party. Draw a floor plan. Describe who was there, when they came, when they left. Try hard to paint a picture of the food table, who was around when Simone keeled over."

Sam nodded. "I was standing right by the food table putting on more California rolls so I can do that. And since I don't smoke pot"—he shot a pointed look at the older members of the team—"my memory is still sharp. But the last time I drew one of these diagrams it didn't help."

"No whining. It could have helped, and it may help this time," Heaven fussed. "Murray, will you take your idea that someone might want to discredit the city or the world of barbeque and run with it? Do some of that creative investigative fancy stuff, okay?"

"You got it," Murray replied.

"What about us?" Joe Long and Chris Snyder pouted.

"You two are assigned the three out-of-town front-runners. Eleazar Martin, Felicity Morgan and Bo Morales. They're from Memphis, Charleston and Amarillo, so you can use the phone at the restaurant for long distance and try to come up with some juicy details. Maybe Felicity stole Aza's wife years ago."

Joe Long was writing furiously on his brand-new steno pad. The actor knew the value of props. Chris was already hatching schemes. "I'll call the barbeque clubs in each town and say I'm, I'm . . ."

"Spare us the details," Heaven said, cutting Chris off at the pass. "Sara, how about spending some more time going over the old employee files?"

"Watch your language," Sara quipped. At fifty-seven, Sara was one of the oldest employees at Cafe Heaven.

"You know what I mean, former employees. See if anyone used a barbeque joint as their reference. Barbara, weren't you in the Dames in Washington, D.C.? Could you call some of your old buddies and see if they have any scoop on Simone? I know she was the national president a few years ago," Heaven asked. The Dames D'Escoffier was an international women's chef association.

Sal looked positively wounded. "I guess you don't need me this time, huh? I guess these fancy schmancy cooks from all over are just outta my league."

Heaven rolled her eyes. "Like we could do anything without you. Please, will you and Mona try to find something out about Ben Franklin, the top-rated contestant at the World Series? He's local, he drives a 1955 Cadillac and he has a mute midget named Mickey as the sole member of his team. Barbara, do you know what Ben does for a living?"

"As a matter of fact, I do kinda. He does something down at the courthouse. Maybe he's an inspector."

Sal padded over to the door and flipped the CLOSED sign

back to OPEN. "The courthouse is my baby. The courthouse I can deal with. We'll know what kind a toilet paper he uses by the time I get done."

Everyone got up to leave. They were talking to their neighbors, and making plans excitedly. Then Joe Long turned as he was leaving. "Boss, what is your assignment?"

"I'll take all the leftovers," Heaven answered. "Dwight Brooks and his new interest in barbeque and the missing recipe are my first stops. And, of course, there's Paul Taylor in all his glory."

Chapter 22

As Heaven made her way across the street, she realized there was a hubbub in front of the cafe. Dwight Brooks was talking to a local news reporter and the camera was rolling.

Well, I guess my first project fell right into my hands, Heaven thought. I'll have to act like I don't care a bit if he's putting his face on TV in front of my restaurant and telling how poor Simone bought the big one. Heaven crossed the street and walked right in the shot, causing everyone to yell.

"Oh, dear. I had no idea you were filming. Dwight, when you get done out here why don't you come in and say hello." Heaven said all this while she kept slowly walking on camera. She couldn't make it easy for some young-thing reporter to make her cafe the talk of the town once again. Heaven continued up the alley to the kitchen door, and, once inside, went over the prep list with the day crew. They were almost done, thank goodness. Heaven didn't feel like concentrating and focusing. Soon the big cowboy hat peeked in the kitchen through the pass-through window from the dining room.

"Heaven, I apologize for not checking with you first, sugar," Dwight said sheepishly.

"Dwight, Simone died here last night. With you or without you there would be cameramen outside today. You might as well get your face on the tube. After all, you have

CDs to sell. By the way, what are you still doing in town?

"Heaven, you do see the big picture, don't you darlin'? I'm not leaving this week. I always planned to stay and eat myself silly. I'm going to try to get Kansas City-style barbeque all figured out for the Smokin' Que."

Heaven didn't really know what she wanted out of Dwight. She needed to get some background on him first. She needed time. But she also wasn't going to let him get away today, even if she wasn't ready for a complete interrogation. She walked over to the pass-through window into the dining room where Dwight's hat was blocking precious daylight. "You know, we have a fun little thing on Monday nights. It's an open-mike show and occasionally when performers are in town over a Monday, they stop by and do a number. Sting and the Indigo Girls and lots of actors have done things. When the Altman movie was in town . . ."

Dwight jumped on top of her lines. "Don't say another word, sugar. What time should I be here?"

Heaven gave him a smile that was at least half sincere. "Nine, nine-thirty?"

"I brought my guitar with me. Now I know why. I'll see you tonight." Dwight did his hat-and-bow trick and disappeared from view.

Pauline and Brian and Robbie cracked up. "Heaven, are you sure the crowd won't think he's a comedy routine? Will they laugh?"

"You couldn't see his tight jeans, Pauline. They will not laugh, trust me. Dwight Brooks is the hottest thing in country music and I do choose my words carefully. I hope Dwight can handle the effect his jeans will have on the gay men in the crowd," Heaven chuckled.

"Heaven, telephone. It's a producer from *Entertainment Tonight*. They're looking for Dwight Brooks. He told them to contact him here. They want a statement about Simone's death in your restaurant."

Heaven wanted to run out the back door and get in the

van and spend the rest of the day at antique malls. She went to the phone instead.

After that phone call, there was another and another, all from various media producers who had been toying with the idea of sending a team to the World Series of Barbeque. They had had their minds made up for them by the untimely death of Simone Springer and a phone call from Dwight Brooks. Heaven told them all that the World Series would be great footage and that she had no idea how Simone died. She had to hand it to old Dwight. No wonder he was hot. He knew how to take advantage of a bad situation. Heaven hadn't done a thing to get ready for the night. Luckily everyone had played around her and as evening came, the place looked pretty good. Joe and Chris came bounding in the kitchen. At the same time Detective Harry Stein did the same thing, slinking instead of bounding. Joe and Chris took one look at the detective and they turned right around and went back the way they came.

"Guess I scared your little fags away, Heaven. They don't like me," Harry said with a sneer.

"What do you want, Detective? You didn't come here to win a popularity contest," Heaven snapped.

"I told Bonnie I'd drop by and let you know how you knocked off your latest victim."

"I don't want to react, but you and I both know I haven't killed anyone, ever. What about Simone?"

"Anaphylactic shock, like the doc thought. Her respiratory system collapsed. Everything constricts: the airways, the blood vessels. Blood escapes into the tissue and you swell up like a pumpkin. The lungs fill up with fluid . . ."

"Stop. This is a kitchen. We have to feed people here. This graphic description is making me sick." Heaven really did feel queasy. "Did the doc figure out what caused this reaction?"

"It was peanuts, all right."

"Detective, am I to understand that Simone died from my sauce?"

"Doc says it was peanuts. He didn't say it was your sauce but you figure it out. She ingested ribs, lots of barbeque sauces, California rolls, wings, noodles. Her stomach was loaded. Everything she ate, you fixed or had your hands on."

"Look, I realize that. It sounds like it was an accident or someone altered Simone's food, someone who knew she was allergic. Of course, she told everyone at the party."

Harry Stein glared across the worktable at Heaven. "Hey, no one pays you to think. Let me take care of that. By the way, did you know old Murray knew Simone in New York? He probably knew all about her allergy."

"So what? Harry, please leave. We have work to do and you're in the way."

"I'll just go to the front and speak to Murray a minute. See you soon, Heaven."

"Oh boy, something to look forward to."

As soon as Harry Stein went to the front of the house, Joe and Chris came back.

"Fill us in," Joe said. Heaven told them what Harry Stein had told her.

"Well, then either she accidently ate some of the peanut sauce or someone slipped it on her plate or in one of the other sauces, maybe the real hot one so she couldn't taste the peanuts." Chris was already brainstorming.

"You've got it, in a nutshell," Joe quipped and all three of them had to laugh.

"Guys, I did something concerning tonight's show that I need to tell you. I asked Dwight Brooks to come sing a song or two." Heaven cringed, waiting for their reaction.

Chris, who had worked the party Sunday night, perked up. "The hunk in the tight jeans?"

"Yes, I know I should have talked it over with you first but it's done and he's coming."

"No problem," Joe said. "We want to tell you about the theme for tonight's show. We think it's brilliant, of course. In honor of the barbeque contest, the theme for tonight's show is meat. I made these fabulous costumes yesterday, so this steak is going to run through the room and be chased by a knife and fork, and a bottle of steak sauce will squirt perfectly harmless colored water on the crowd and there will be . . .''

"I get it, I get it," Heaven said. "Just don't think you can recreate Pigpen's demise in the stockpot. It's just too soon."

Chris and Joe looked at each other. "Okay, but we reserve the right to do it at the end of the year when we do our 'Ten Best News Stories of the Year show,' " Chris offered.

"Agreed," Heaven said.

Now there was some uncomfortable shifting. Chris poked Joe. Joe continued. "What would a meat show be, Heaven, without a little homage to the penis?"

"I'm not going to argue the premise. A meat show has to have an homage to the penis, I guess. A tasteful little bohemian poem about the names you guys call your, eh, would be just fine. I think given what you've just told me, you should let Dwight Brooks go on first, special guest star, blah, blah. Then you go for the meat, so to speak." She went to the pass-through and yelled for Murray.

"What's up, babe?"

"Is Harry still here?" Heaven asked.

"No. Our conversation didn't take very long. Harry was angling for me and Simone having an affair in our old lives in New York, the old poke-the-neighbor trick, scores to settle, revenge. You know the number."

"So?" Heaven noticed that Murray's eyes were full of tears.

"So I explained to the guy how I felt about my Eva. And he left."

"Somehow I think you're leaving out the best part, like how you told him to shove it, but that's okay, we all like to have our private triumphs. Murray, I just want you to know, these wacky guys are doing a meat show tonight and

I did not say it was okay for anyone to show their meat. And you two, get outta the kitchen.''

Joe and Chris scampered for the dining room. Murray stayed, looking in at Heaven from the pass-through.

"Good call. No sense showing your meat in the nineties. You can't do anything with it once it's out.'' He turned back toward the dining room.

Heaven felt terrible that something she made might have killed Simone. She was preoccupied through the busy dinner, she was preoccupied when Dwight Brooks came and did a wonderful thirty-minute set to a standing ovation. She barely laughed when the kids did a rollicking version of *The Cook, the Thief, His Wife and Her Lover* with a barbeque contest twist. The only time she came out of herself was when, in a feeble attempt to extract information from Dwight Brooks, she went out to the bar and had a drink with him. She had a glass of Côte du Rhône, he had a margarita.

Heaven hit the jackpot with her first question, which went something like, "How did you and Simone Springer know each other, Dwight?"

To which Dwight Brooks replied, "Oh, I thought you knew. We used to be married."

Bingo.

Chapter 23

Once in a while, brilliance strikes, Heaven thought. Today, when I remembered Cork Stuecheck, I was inspired. I hope he can shed some light on this whole barbeque world. If anyone knows about it, it's him.

Heaven pulled onto a gravel path that led back to a huge wooden frame house hidden by big shade trees. The house was now surrounded by housing developments, but it and the twenty-five acres it sat on would never be the site of faux French country estates. At least, not as long as Cork Stuecheck was alive. Cork had inherited the house and the land from his grandfather. It was near Olathe, Kansas, a town that used to be twenty miles from the hubbub of Kansas City. Now it was considered only a mid-point suburb. There were miles of new houses beyond it, but they weren't on Cork's land.

Heaven had met Cork at the Kansas City Art Institute, where her third husband had taught painting. Cork had taught painting too, and was a student favorite. One of the things that made him popular were his spectacular cookouts. Cork was a backyard cooker supreme. Heaven could still taste his smoked chicken stuffed with homemade sausage and apples. At everyone's urging, Cork got involved with the Barbeque Guild when it was a fledgling organization. He was still famous in barbeque lore for doing his smoking in old kitchen stoves. At the American Royal contest, he would have three or four old stoves lined up with fires built in the bottom of them and meat nestled in the ovens. When the contests were over he let a used-appliance company come and pick them up. He always got new old stoves for each contest and said it kept him from getting too attached to the "tools." Cork won the Grand Championship at the American Royal several times in the seventies and early eighties. His all-night vigils around the stoves were legendary. Art students and food people spent the night drinking and solving the world's problems. When the prize money got too big and the rules got too numerous, Cork stopped entering contests. Heaven remembered some big fight. Now she wished she'd paid more attention. Who knew barbeque gossip would be so important to her well-being someday?

Heaven had lost touch with Cork but she knew that he had recently retired from the Art Institute. When she called him, he teased her about the TV coverage of Simone's death and asked her to come for lunch. Tuesday being the slow day at the cafe that it was, Heaven said yes. Now she was knocking on Cork's door and he was opening it with a smile and a hug to greet her.

Cork was an Ichabod Crane sort of a guy, tall and thin with a big Adam's apple and bigger nose. His long gray hair was pulled back in a ponytail. All the parts seemed wrong but the whole package was totally charming. Heaven felt right at home, as if the last time she had seen Cork had been last week instead of five years ago.

"I thought we would have a distinctly non-barbeque lunch," Cork said with a twinkle in his eyes. "I made a risotto with some nice shiitakes. And we have a great bottle of white Burgundy that I've been saving for the right occasion."

Lunch with Cork was the most pleasant two hours Heaven had spent in a while. The food was delicious, the conversation intelligent and the background material on the barbeque world invaluable to Heaven.

When she left she was more confused than she had been when she arrived.

She drove north and east to the guild office in Raytown. There was something that Stephanie didn't know to ask about so Heaven decided to check it out herself.

Joyce, the secretary at the Barbeque Guild office, couldn't have been nicer. Another lady from the Que Queens had called her today, she said, inquiring about the judges. She, Joyce, had been at a wedding in Wichita over the weekend and hadn't been around for all the action. What a time to be out of town, she said. Heaven asked her if she and Stephanie had worked things out and if she had been able to answer Stephanie's questions. "Oh, yeah, but I'm sorry if me telling who was going to be out at the kitchen caused any trouble. I can't even remember telling anyone in particular but it had never . . ."

"Don't worry about that. What's done is done. I wanted to ask you about something else. Will you walk me through the whole process of keeping track of whose entry is whose?" Heaven asked in her most winsome way.

"No problem. When the team sends in their entry fee, they are assigned a number. When they come to the contest, they check in and they are given the Styrofoam containers for every entry. These containers each have a different number. When contestants bring their entries to the judges' station on the day of a contest, these numbers are changed by putting a sticker over the first number with another number. That way the judges don't know anything," the secretary said brightly.

Heaven was jotting all this down. "So next to the name of the team is their entry number, then next to that are the numbers of the containers that are checked out to them, then next to the numbers of the containers are the numbers that the numbers of the containers were changed to, correct?"

"Yes, correct."

"So the judges don't know who is who but anyone who had access to that list would know, wouldn't they? Or they could figure it out. Do the members of the committee who enter the scores into the computer have the list?''

The secretary looked confused. She had never thought of it like that. ''No, the volunteers just scan in the judges' ballots and then the computer prints out a list of the standings. They, the judges, never see the original team numbers.''

''But,'' Heaven pushed on, ''someone has to take the original team numbers and the list of standings and find out who won, don't they?''

''That would be me.''

Heaven wanted to snap her head off. ''But you were not there this weekend so who did it instead of you, dear?''

''That would be Paul Taylor, the guild president.''

''Thank you so much,'' Heaven said as she headed for the door. ''One more thing. Do you keep all these lists?''

The secretary nodded proudly. ''For one year.''

When Heaven got back to the restaurant she grabbed the phone and called Bonnie Weber. By a stroke of luck, the detective was in her office.

Heaven was behind a day in reporting her news to the authorities. ''Did you know that Dwight Brooks was once married to Simone Springer?''

''How did *you* know that?''

''He told me last night. He came over and did a set at the open mike. We had a drink together and he just casually mentioned it. Said he thought I would know that. I couldn't tell him I had never had an interest in his life before now.''

Bonnie sighed. ''Well, his bio did say he was married in 1984 and divorced in 1988. But I didn't see Simone's name in the press kit that his record company faxed me. I also found that little tidbit out, but from the Simone side of the family. Her brother in California.''

''How did it come up?''

Bonnie chortled. ''What do you want? An office down here? I shouldn't tell you another morsel, but I shot off a list of names to the brother and asked him if he had heard his sister mention any of these people. You were on that list, by the way. Dwight's name made the brother almost go into orbit.''

''I'm embarrassed I didn't know about this cross-cultural match. I guess even I don't know everything about every woman chef.''

''I can't believe you would admit anything less than know all, see all. Dwight was a 'family tragedy,' as the brother put it. He was adamant about not wanting to talk about it. I'm going to find out, of course. Do you think Murray will know?''

''He would be a very good place to start. Do you have his number?''

''Yeah,'' Bonnie said. ''Heaven, I know you guys were planning one of your sessions of detecting at Sal's on Monday.''

''And?''

''And I want to come to the next get-together.''

''Thursday. I'll let you know when. Why are you not yelling at me, telling me to mind my own business?''

''I'll save it for Thursday. Heaven, I'm concerned about your welfare. Do you know that you're one of the things . . .''

''That both of the victims have in common. Plus I was around when I was shot at. I know. But I just happened to find Pigpen and Simone just happened to be here when she was, you know. I didn't really know either one of them.''

Bonnie's voice was rising in decibels. ''There are very few coincidences in my business, H. Will you just cool it until I've had a chance to do my job? Please?''

''Oh, gosh, I hear the kitchen calling me. Bye, Bonnie,'' Heaven said and hung up the phone quickly. She had more work to do.

So did Bonnie. She was working on a theory today, the theory that if there was one connection between the players in this Barbeque and Murder saga, there could be more connections. If two barbeque judges from two totally different professions and countries of residence had been married to each other, there might be other strange and zany facts to be uncovered. Bonnie had the list of judges, the list of teams, the list of the World Series contest committee and, of course, the Kansas City Barbeque Guild membership list. A database expert downstairs was working on all the lists of names and addresses. Bonnie didn't expect much from this first matchup but she had to start somewhere. So far her famous legal pads were pretty bare. The MOTIVE pad was the fullest under the Pigpen heading. She had written:

1. missing recipe could have been stolen and could be worth some money
2. revenge for cheating at a contest or just winning a contest that someone else wanted to win
3. screwed someone in a plumbing deal

Under the Simone heading, Bonnie was lost. She didn't know much about the woman. Yesterday she had called the newspaper for all the clips they had on Simone Springer. They had made them available, Bonnie had sent someone for them and had even read them. Simone seemed a successful woman. The only clues Bonnie had to go on was her relationship with Dwight and her friendship with Murray. On the motive page, Bonnie had:

1. Dwight seeking revenge for a failed marriage
2. professional jealousy
3. does Murray have a motive?

Even she thought this last one was far-fetched but she had to put it to paper. That's how she problem-solved. Bonnie was meeting Murray for coffee on the Plaza in an hour. She was hoping for some insight into Simone. Then she was going to visit with Mrs. Paul Taylor, who insisted her husband was with her all afternoon last Tuesday. Don't these people work? she thought.

Bonnie dropped the MOTIVE pad and picked up the OP-PORTUNITY pad. Anyone could have come into that commissary kitchen, hit and then pushed an unconscious Pigpen into that pot. Knowing that he always mixed up the sauce alone made it easy to invent all kind of scenarios. Even though Pigpen was hefty, it wasn't impossible to see a woman doing it. Certainly a group of women could pull it off easily. But Bonnie could not take seriously the possibility that the Que Queens were so involved in their charity work that they would kill someone to get more barbeque votes. It was also hard to place any of the barbeque competitors that really might want to eliminate Hopkins as a major contender in Kansas City on that Tuesday. Anyone but Ben Franklin, that is. Ben had really benefited by Pigpen's demise. On the OPPORTUNITY pad, under Pigpen, Bonnie had jotted: Que Queens, Ben Franklin, team members, Paul Taylor. Under Simone, there was the cryptic line: Everyone at that damn party. Bonnie didn't like the OPPOR-TUNITY pad and she threw it at the wall opposite her desk. The MEANS pad didn't warrant a glance. Nothing new there. One victim had drowned in his own sauce, one had respiratory failure due to peanuts. This food theme was making Bonnie hungry. She took off for the Plaza to meet Murray and have a snack.

Chapter 24

"Murray, I know this is hard for you. But try to help. Whatever you tell me will be our little secret. Does Simone have something in her past that would make someone trick her into eating peanuts? What was she like when you were neighbors in New York?" Detective Bonnie Weber had an iced mocha latte in one hand and a scone in the other.

"It's the secret part that's making me twitchy," Murray grumbled. "Heaven would be disappointed if I knew something and told you and didn't tell the team. Simone was between husbands when we lived next to each other. I remember her saying her ex had been a musician but until Heaven told me last night I didn't know it was Dwight. Or if I did know she'd been married to a Dwight, it sure didn't connect with Dwight Brooks. I introduced her to her second husband, another reporter. She would cook these incredible meals and we'd bring the wine and once in a while I'd invite someone from the office. This one Sunday we invited this guy from the editorial desk who had just gotten divorced and Simone and he really hit it off. He was ten, fifteen years older than her. When he got an offer from the *Washington Post* about a year later, they got married and moved to Washington together. That was about six months before Eva was killed. I kinda lost touch. I lost touch with everybody," Murray said quietly.

"Did you know that Simone and the *Washington Post* had gotten divorced?" Bonnie asked.

"To tell you the truth, I hadn't thought about Simone for years. Or him. But I did read in the paper that she was one of the celebs coming in for the big grill-off and I was looking forward to seeing her again. On Saturday, we got together for a drink at the Ritz after the contest. That's when she filled me in. Seems like she'd been doing real well."

"Murray, did she say anything about Dwight Brooks, like, 'Isn't this a coincidence, my ex-husband is a judge too?' Or, 'By the way, I think someone wants to kill me?' "

"Not a word, Bonnie. Not a word."

Mrs. Paul Taylor was a nice enough lady, pretty, in her late forties, Bonnie guessed. She had asked Bonnie if she wanted coffee, saying it wouldn't take a minute. Bonnie had said yes. Lots of people were more comfortable talking to a police officer if they had something to do with their hands, Bonnie had discovered.

"Do you participate in the barbeque contests, Mrs. Taylor?" Bonnie had noticed lots of couples working together over the weekend.

"No," Mrs. Taylor said quickly. "I used to, but then we had the kids, and Paul said it was just too much trouble to pack everyone up."

"How old are your children?" Bonnie asked as she looked around the kitchen for signs of high chairs or sports equipment.

"We have a girl in her second year of college at MU, then a boy still in high school, a junior." Mrs. Taylor was busy at the sink.

Bonnie decided not to dick around anymore. She didn't have time for this small talk. "You told me you were with your husband all day last Tuesday, the day Pigpen died. I take it you don't work or you both took the day off or what?"

"We both work out of here, out of the house," Mrs.

Taylor said defensively. "Paul is a real estate agent. He has an office in Overland Park but he's been at it for twenty-two years so he can pretty much work on his own. He has a fax and answering machine and all in the basement. I have a craft business. I make dried wreaths and flower arrangements. I have the other half of the basement."

"How cozy," Bonnie said dryly. "What's the beef between your husband and Pigpen? I hear they used to be on the same team, they had a big fight? Do you know what your husband was doing frisking the dead body the other day? I saw you at the back of the crowd at the cemetery. Surely you . . . ."

Mrs. Taylor slammed down the coffeepot on its warmer. She brought two full cups over to the table and sat down, her eyes avoiding Bonnie's gaze. She was skittish, all right, Bonnie thought. "Surely you have some ideas about why your husband was so, impetuous?"

As she drank her coffee, Mrs. Taylor's hand was shaking. "Dewayne was not a very nice man but I went to the funeral with Paul out of respect for his wife. We used to see each other, back in the days when everyone on the circuit was cooking just for the love of it. Paul and Dewayne came up with that sauce recipe together. And somehow, when they had a falling out, Dewayne ended up with it. The worst thing is that he would tease Paul about it. Last year, *Gourmet* did a big piece about barbeque and they rated the ten best sauces in the country and Dewayne's was number six. He sent that article to Paul with the parts about him highlighted and the words, 'This could be you, chump,' scrawled across it."

"I bet that made your husband mad, didn't it?" Bonnie said smoothly. "What do you mean, somehow Dewayne ended up with it? Don't you know what happened?"

"Paul never would talk about it. But I think it just festered and he went haywire last Friday. He won't talk about that either. Says to just forget it."

"Sometimes that's easier said than done, eh, Mrs. Taylor.

By the way, has your husband ever mentioned Simone Springer? She's the chef who . . .''

"Oh, I know who she is. I have one of her cookbooks. And yes, she had called here several times. I talked to her. I think she and Paul had a meeting on Sunday.''

Bonnie Weber wanted to do a tap dance. "That would be last Sunday before the party at Heaven's?''

Mrs. Taylor was either totally thick or she had her own agenda. "Yes," she nodded, "before she died.''

Cork Stuecheck tromped through the woods, pulling a wheelbarrel loaded with a chainsaw behind him. The trees were starting to lose leaves but it was still beautiful out there, lots of gold and red. There was nothing like a little physical labor to clear your head, Cork told himself. All this barbeque business had got him upset; he hadn't slept much the last couple of nights. He had been glad to talk to Heaven about history, but Pigpen's death and the other one, the woman, had really caused him to think about the old days.

He had been a pretty darn good cooker. Pigpen and Paul had both admitted he could outcook them on a given day. Thinking about all this, he had to admit two things. He missed it and he was still mad as hell.

Might as well use that anger to cut some wood. One of the best things about this farm was how he had been able to plant the kinds of hardwood trees he loved to cook with right on his own place. For the past few years, he'd just been using them for firewood instead of slow cooking meat, but he was still proud of the oaks, the cherry, the hickory and a few of the more exotic woods that he had on his own land. Cork was headed for the back part of his property. He'd feel better after a good hike and some work with the chainsaw. He'd fill up the wheelbarrel a few times. That should tucker him out. Maybe he'd made a mistake retiring this year. He just had too much time to think.

*　　*　　*

Heaven's head flopped over to one side. She woke with a start. Oh, boy, sleeping in your car in Raytown, she thought. That's what happens when I try to be quiet for twenty minutes. She checked her watch. It was close to six and the fall dusk had set in. Heaven looked across the street and down a quarter of a block, at the small freestanding building that housed the Barbeque Guild. "I wish she would go home. I've got more to do tonight than some silly stakeout," Heaven mumbled. As if on cue, the guild's secretary, the very one that had been so nice this afternoon, came out and hopped in her car. "It's about time. Jack, are you ready?"

Jumpin' Jack was sitting silently beside Heaven in the van. Either he was ill at ease about being away from Thirty-ninth Street, or he was in his surveillance mode. Of course he was attired in ninja black with some black face paint on. He turned toward Heaven and actually smiled. "Ready when you are, H." Jack held up a SlimJim, the device that auto clubs use to open locked doors, in one hand. In the other hand was a lock-picking set.

As Heaven and Jack pulled into the small parking lot at the side of the guild office, Heaven had a moment of guilt. The morality of using a well-meaning but unstable friend to break into a building and steal records was iffy at best. The moment passed and Heaven reminded herself that Jack wanted to help, just like everyone else did. His skills were unique in the group. How could she not use that which he practiced so diligently?

"I tried to check it out today when I was here. I don't think there's an alarm. They probably don't get too many thieves looking for barbeque contest notices or contest ballots," Heaven said as they got out of the van and headed for the door.

"I noticed the subject did not lock the door with a key," Jack said officially. "This indicates no dead bolt. Please stay here. Let me check the back," he said as he disappeared around the corner.

Heaven glanced around. There was a small strip mall next

door that was filled mostly with closed offices. A hair salon still had a couple of cars in front of it and a pet food shop seemed to be doing a thriving business. No one was looking over at the little building. Suddenly the front door opened and Jack stood there beaming.

"Madam," he bowed. Heaven slipped in quickly. She had a big flashlight and a magnifying glass in her purse. "OK, Jack. Take off in the van. I don't want Paul Taylor or someone else from the committee to cruise by here and recognize it. Come back for me in an hour."

"I don't want to leave you here alone," Jack said valiantly.

"Then take the van up the street and stash it and come back in and be still. Earlier today I saw where they kept the records from last year's contests. I'm going to do as much as I can in one hour, then we better go. I don't want to tempt fate too much." Heaven was already digging in a file cabinet while she bossed Jack around. Her stomach was doing flips. She was excited. If two people hadn't been murdered lately, this would be fun.

Fifty minutes later, Heaven yelped. Jack, who was plastered against the front wall, SWAT-team style, peering through the blinds, jumped into a combat stance. "Sorry," Heaven said. "I didn't mean to scare you. I finally found something big. But this doesn't make sense."

"Did you find evidence of foul play?" Jack asked seriously.

Heaven flipped the switch on the copy machine. "Oh, yeah. I'm going to just copy this stuff and figure it out in the privacy of my own home. Jack, will you get our chariot? I'll be out in two minutes."

"Be back in five," Jack said as he slid out the front door.

Within an hour and five minutes, Heaven had deposited Jack at the restaurant with instructions to feed him and had run home with her ill-gotten spoils. Before the shower water was hot, Heaven heard the front door. Hank ran up the stairs.

"Why, look what's happened. Without even planning it,

we're home before midnight, together," Heaven said from the bathroom. "Will you join me in a . . ."

Hank appeared in the bathroom door, his hospital greens in his hand. The bedroom light made a halo around his bare body. "Yes. Whatever you're offering, I want."

"Then I'm going to have to think of something special," Heaven said as she took off her own black SWAT-style T-shirt and tights. "Come here."

In another hour and five minutes, Heaven and Hank sat in bed with the stolen papers. "This is sure better than an after-sex cigarette," Hank teased as he kissed Heaven on her neck. "After-sex stolen secrets. I know it would be totally futile to tell you that you shouldn't have broken into the office. A shot fired into your car didn't stop you, so I know I can't stop you. What did you steal?"

Heaven tried to look sheepish for a minute. At least she could give him that. The minute over, she started to point out salient details. "I learned today how they keep track of the scores for the barbeque contests. It's very complicated but the punch line is that Paul Taylor changed the scores last weekend. He also changed some other scores from during the year. But I would have bet the farm that he would have changed scores to benefit Pigpen."

"The dead guy?"

"Yeah. I was sure that Pigpen was blackmailing Paul."

"But what does that have to do with last weekend? Pigpen was already dead last weekend," Hank pointed out as he kissed Heaven's foot.

The kissing was making Heaven forget her place. "Well, my second choice for blackmailers would have been the front-runners: Bo or Felicity or Aza. But that isn't who the contest was rigged for."

"And the winner is?" Hank asked as he worked his way up Heaven's leg.

"Ben Franklin. Paul, or someone, but I think it's Paul, changed a bunch of scores. Now Ben didn't win that many contests this season, but Friday night he was the second top scorer overall in the guild for the season. Then on Saturday he was on top for the World Series. And that score was definitely jimmied, the totals are much more than the sum of the parts.''

"And you wonder, why Ben?''

"I certainly do.'' Heaven swept all the papers on the floor with one fell swoop and rolled over on top of Hank. "But I'm not going to find the answer tonight. I love you, Hank.''

"And I love you, H. Please be careful, for me.''

Chapter 25

Heaven put down the phone. She knew she should have gone through Bonnie Weber for this. Technically, asking someone to hack into the phone company computer must be against several laws. But compared to the breaking and entering of last night, this was peanuts.

Heaven herself was not capable of electronic crime, but she had a friend who was an electronic graphic designer and he loved sticking his nose where it didn't belong. The idea here was that there might be a record of some phone contact between Dwight and Simone before they got to town. Dwight told Heaven that he hadn't seen or talked to Simone in years but that he did know she was going to be in Kansas City. Heaven wanted to see if Dwight was telling the truth. While she was at it, she asked for the last month in the telephone lives of Felicity, Aza and Bo. Might as well go all the way. Her friend said he would get back to her this evening.

Now it was time to find something cute to wear. Heaven was meeting Felicity for lunch. They were going to the Classic Cup in Westport and since Heaven didn't get to go out to lunch much, she wanted to be suited up for it properly. Confusion in the closet ensued. When Heaven emerged, she was in her usual black tights but with the beautiful Italian high heels in place of her black Reeboks. She slipped a short black leather skirt over her tights. A black long-sleeved Gap

T-shirt and a black vintage suit jacket completed the ensemble. Heaven made a few notes and took off for midtown.

Even without her entourage of head turners, Felicity June Morgan stopped traffic. Heaven was already at their table when Felicity got to the cafe so she was able to see the whole thing. The beautiful blonde was in a creamy ivory suit, probably Bill Blass or Armani. She sat down and patted Heaven's hand. "Honey, I bet you wish this li'l ol' barbeque contest had never come to town. What a mess."

Heaven laughed. "Yeah, you guys are a barrel of laughs. Felicity, what made you get involved in hardwood cooking?" That was Heaven's favorite term for the process.

"I went to a contest in Beaufort, South Carolina, in 1980. I was young and rich and didn't have a goddamn thing to think about. These people, there were only about thirty teams, were having a ball. I went right out and bought a recreational vehicle, a smoker, a trailer, the whole works. At first, I wouldn't even enter my product. I'd just pay the entry fee and cook, trying to imitate what everyone else was doing. When I finally entered my meat, I started winning. Been winning since."

"I talked to a friend of mine yesterday and he said to say hello to you. Cork Stuecheck," Heaven said. "Cork has great stories of those early years before the prize money and the egos got big, as Cork put it."

Felicity smiled. "Cork always had a way with words and the paintbrush. I have one of his paintings in my dining room in Charleston. I wish he and Paul Taylor hadn't had such a fight and that Cork was still contest cooking."

"What exactly did they fight about? Cork said it was philosophical differences."

"Philosophical differences and a woman, a particularly deadly combination."

Heaven shook her head. "Felicity, please don't use the term 'deadly combination' this week. Do you know who the woman was that Paul and Cork fought over?"

Felicity waved for the waiter. "I sure do, sugar. It was me. I'm starved. Let's order."

Heaven had to hand it to Felicity. Her timing and delivery were impeccable. They ordered a bottle of barrel-fermented Newton Chardonnay to go with their food. The talk drifted to cuisine in general and then the source of Felicity's wealth. "Felicity, what did your family do to make money?"

"Shipping. My great-great-grandfather was a robber baron up and down the coasts of Georgia and Carolina. Brought fine furniture and stuff from England. Took hemp and indigo back. He made a ton of money. My grandfather and daddy didn't fuck up and gamble it away. They even made some more. My parents are still alive, still having parties for the Charleston Historical Society. But I've had my own slice of the money since I was eighteen."

"Do your parents know that you have an alternative life-style?"

"My parents don't want any unnecessary details. Am I in good health? Will I come to dinner when the Merrills are in town? Do I want to go to Paris in the spring? They do not want to know who I'm having sex with, male or female."

"Speaking of that, what do I have to promise you to get the story about you and Cork and Paul?"

Felicity grinned a nasty grin. "I can see you're getting the picture. Nothing comes for free in the barbeque contest world. But, just to show you what a great person I am, I'll tell you this story, no strings attached. In the old days, there was no money involved in this barbeque world, so that left sex as the prime topic of interest, besides cooking, of course. You're at Memphis in May and it's late at night and everybody is all liquored up, and, well, things happen."

"Sounds familiar."

"Well, I was a very bad girl and didn't care if someone was married or not in those days. I was married myself, to a weak-kneed boy from Duke. Paul and Cork were married too, but that didn't keep them from jumping in my Winnebago when they got the chance,'' Felicity said with a wry grimace.

"I'm assuming not at the same time. In the Winnebago, I mean. Jumping.''

Felicity gave Heaven a look that told her threesomes were not completely out of the question. "Well, not at the absolute same time but at the same time generally. That was the problem. Paul finally tried to beat up Cork, told him he was leaving his wife so he and I could be together. Told Cork to get out of my life and not show his face at a contest again. I was furious with Paul. Told him I had no intention of leaving my husband for anyone, but if I was leaving my husband, it would be for Cork, not him. Cork wouldn't speak to either one of us. He didn't have a clue I was slutting around the contest circuit until Paul told him.''

"Have you all kissed and made up?'' Heaven asked.

"Paul and I have, of course. We see each other three or four times a year at contests. I've never seen Cork again.''

"You're kidding. Well, Felicity, you sure did raise some hell. As long as we're telling tales out of school, how about filling me in on some of the pertinent info on your competition,'' Heaven ventured.

"Sugar, you know I'm surrounded by mean ol' boys. Eleazar has a wife who's divorcing him, two kids in college and another still in high-school. He has his work cut out for him. Other than that, as much as I hate to say it, Aza is a good guy. I have never seen him be unkind and I have seen him do things to help other cookers. I like him. Bo Morales is an ambitious little fucker with a gimmick. If he doesn't win this year, he will next year, or the year after that. Pigpen Hopkins was the worst. He hated having a woman as a contender. He hated having a black and a Hispanic as contenders. He was the kind of guy who cheats at golf and uses inferior pipes in his plumbing jobs. Two years ago, Pigpen really showed his true colors when he poisoned one of Bo's mules. Then there was the time he got drunk in Baton Rouge and pissed in my smoking chamber. On my ribs. We didn't like ol' Pigpen a bit.''

Heaven laughed. ''Neither did we. When we started having these battles of the sexes, it was because Pigpen went on record, in the paper or somewhere, that women couldn't cook. A radio station picked up on it and we called in and said we would take the challenge but it had to benefit our favorite charity, the Food Bank. Every time the men's team won, Pigpen came up with another more insulting quote.''

Felicity eyed Heaven slyly. ''Then you just happened to be the one who found him in the sauce. Come on now, you can tell me. Did you do us all a favor?''

Heaven laughed. ''No way. I've done some dumb things in my life but I wouldn't knock someone out cold, drown them and then discover them and call it in myself. There are ways to commit murder that don't put the spotlight right on the guilty party, you know.''

''Does that knowledge come from experience?''

''Yes, experience in the field of law, not murder. I was an attorney.''

''And you gave it up for the love of food?''

''Actually, it gave me up.''

Felicity emptied her wine glass and refilled. ''What else are you keepin' from me, sugar? What other good stories are up your sleeve?''

''Other than that, I've been a saint.''

''Oh, yeah. How many husbands and name them.''

Heaven could feel the beginning of a blush. ''Boy, you're a tough interview. Okay. Number One, Sandy Martin. Number Two—''

''Wait, I didn't ask it right,'' Felicity said. ''I want to add something, give me a sentence description of the man and the marriage.''

''Sandy Martin was my high-school sweetheart. He's a lawyer here in Kansas City. Roger McGuinne is . . .''

Felicity interrupted again. ''The rock star?''

''Yes, he and I have a child, Iris McGuinne. Then came

Ian Wolff, the famous painter. He broke my heart and ran off with a Brazilian performance artist. Sol Steinberg owned a uniform company here in town. He was a dear man and had a heart attack and died. Jason Kelley is a designer and architect. We got married. I opened the restaurant, we got divorced. There you have it. Gosh, Felicity, I sound a lot more interesting than I really am.''

"You've had variety in your men. I like that in a woman,'' Felicity said.

"What about you? What happened to the weak-kneed husband from Duke? Are there others?''

"I paid him off and divorced him years ago. He became very tedious very quickly. I only married that one time. About the time I got in trouble with Paul and Cork, I lost interest in boys. Girls are much more fun. You should try it sometime, Heaven.''

Heaven got up. She had already arranged to pay the check later. "Who says I haven't? This is my town and my treat. Thanks for all the delicious background material on everyone, your own self included. I've got to get to work. See you Friday.''

"Heaven, you're a kick, sugar. Thanks for lunch.'' Felicity got up and kissed Heaven full on the mouth. The Classic Cup customers were captivated. Heaven could see Charlene Welling, the owner, laughing and rolling her eyes back of the cheese counter, pointing in Heaven's direction.

Heaven had ten minutes to get to her next appointment. She shot over to Cafe Heaven, ran in the kitchen to make sure they were doing okay on the prep list and then made a fresh pot of coffee.

Paul Taylor walked in the front door. Heaven greeted him like an old friend. "Thanks for coming over, Paul. I feel like we need to talk. I made some coffee. It's espresso roast, Columbian and Kenya AA blended.''

Paul had no idea what she was talking about. "I guess it isn't Folger's,'' he said nervously as he took a full cup from Heaven. They sat down at a table in the empty dining room.

Heaven pulled out her note cards. "Paul, what is going on? This is all too weird. Let me just go through the last week or so. First, Pigpen dies and you come out and stay with us and you were very supportive that night. Then last Thursday you sneak in when I'm not looking and . . ."

"Heaven, I didn't know you were there, honestly."

"OK, we'll go with that. You were looking for the recipe because Pigpen's teammates couldn't find it, correct?"

Paul nodded yes.

"Of course, that was the same night that I was shot at by someone who knew where I was going to be, going north in my van downtown. On Friday, you made a total fool of yourself at the funeral. Now Paul, don't squirm. On Friday you actually were so desperate, you snuck into a hearse and looked through the pockets of a corpse. And got caught, I might add. Friday night, your wife wouldn't let you out of the house. She was afraid for your sanity. On Saturday, you cooked like shit. It's a good thing it was just for charity 'cause you would have been in last place. On Sunday, Simone Springer died in this very place we're sitting. And you were here, of course. Now you have to admit that when you hear the highlights, just the facts, sir, it sounds fishy. You haven't been yourself since Pigpen died. Paul, I know you and I are hardly more than acquaintances but we've been through all these things together in the last eight days. What's the deal?"

Paul got up and started pacing. "A lot changed after Pigpen died."

"What changed, Paul? Please tell me what changed."

"Pigpen's sauce recipe, the one that he's won so many awards with. I was one of his partners in developing that sauce. We had a legal agreement. I got a check from him every six months. His lawyer sent it to my lawyer. My name wasn't on the label but that deal was okay with me until Dewayne died. For a variety of reasons. I never had a copy of the recipe. I was dumb, I guess, not to insist on a copy, but Dewayne was calling the shots. When Dewayne died, his team called. They were frantic. I told them what I remembered about the ingredients and they made up a batch that got them through the weekend. I wasn't quite right, I know that. I musta forgot something important. I'm gonna have to work on it, if we can't find the recipe, that is.

"Anyhow, on Friday, I started drinking as soon as I got up. I believed that Dewayne had screwed me as usual, that we would never find the recipe. I was also suspicious that he had sold the recipe and cut me out. That he'd made a deal that I wasn't a part of. I thought crazy thoughts. Of course by the time I got to the cemetery I was sure Pigpen was taking the recipe with him just for meanness. Of course, I know Dewayne didn't know he was going to check out last week, and I also know that his wife had to provide the overalls he was . . . I got crazy."

Paul paused and gulped air. "There's more. I was right about Dewayne making a deal. Someone contacted me. They were willing to pay through the nose for that sauce recipe. They said Pigpen was willing to sell it and cut me out of the deal, just like I thought, so why should I worry about his family? I tried to find it but I failed."

"I guess my two questions are, first, who wants to buy the sauce recipe and, second, you said partners in the plural. You and Dewayne and . . ." Heaven asked softly. Maybe this is where Ben Franklin comes in. Heaven wasn't willing to mention the rigged scores to Paul today.

"Not yet. I'm not ready to give up yet, Heaven. I'll tell you that when I'm sure I can't sell the recipe."

"I thought you didn't find the recipe, Paul? Are you sure you didn't find something when you went through the casket?"

"I haven't found the recipe. That's the truth."

"One last question, Paul, why was Pigpen calling the shots?"

"Because he was a blackmailing bastard, Heaven, and

that's all I'm gonna say.'' With that Paul Taylor walked out of the restaurant.

"Good delivery. He left me on the edge of my seat," Heaven said as she went off to the kitchen.

Chapter 26

Getting restaurant people up and talking before nine in the morning was not easy.

It was eight-thirty and here they all were. Sal's barber shop was full. Heaven had picked up Lamar's donuts, Sara had brought freshly squeezed orange and apple juice, and the waiters had brought attitudes. Bonnie Weber was there as she had requested. Heaven banged some scissors on a bottle of hair tonic to call the meeting to order.

"Here we go. As you can see, Bonnie Weber is sitting in this morning. I'm sure she will share with us later. In the meantime, let's share with her. Do we have anything to share? Sara?"

Sara shook her head. "I struck out. I guess it's not a surprise that no one used a barbeque joint as a reference to get a job at Cafe Heaven, but so far, I've done two years, and I haven't come across any reference to barbeque at all. We did have a bartender from Nashville once but that's it."

Heaven looked at Murray, who was sitting next to Sara. "What about you, Murray?"

"I called the mayor's assistant, good ol' Nolan, and he got back to me yesterday. There hasn't been a threat to the mayor or the city generally in months. The irate letter writers are the same ones that have been writing irate letters since the mayor was elected.

"Then I called the press officer at the police station.

Vince somebody. He told me they had no particular threats that had come in for the barbeque series. They were doing their patrol as usual. The committee had hired security for the venue and the health department was keeping an eye on the contest. The city seemed more concerned that people would get sick from food poisoning than anything else. If there's a political mad-bomber type who killed Pigpen and Simone, he or she hasn't claimed credit for either death.''

Heaven felt the tightness in the pit of her stomach that told her they weren't getting anywhere. Stephanie was next. ''Stephanie, what about the Barbeque Guild?''

Stephanie put down her emery board to give her report. The sound of filing had almost put her in harm's way from Murray and Joe Long. Joe quickly grabbed the offending tool as soon as it was released from Stephanie's hand, hiding it under his chair. ''The secretary out at the guild office was very sweet. She said lots of times people call up and say, for instance, do you have the kitchen rented on next Thursday? And she looks at the clipboard with the schedule on it, and then she might tell the person on the other end of the phone, yes, the Bilardo Brothers have it all day, or, Flower of the Flames is using it from ten to two. It never occurred to her to not tell someone on the phone who has reserved the space. On the other hand, she doesn't specifically remember telling anyone that Pigpen was going to be making sauce last Tuesday or that the Que Queens were due out there Tuesday night. Yet she did have to admit someone could very easily have obtained that information from the guild office. The bad news is that no one called up and made an impression on the secretary, by being weird or scary or asking too many questions about Pigpen or something like that. Now, on to the judges.

''The Barbeque Guild has a whole roster of judges that have taken the judges' certification test. This list gets an invitation to judge the American Royal every year and they also get invited to judge the World Series. The catch is, the American Royal needs between two and three hundred judges and the World Series just needs around fifty the first weekend and double that the second. So they got more responses than they needed, and ended up drawing names out of a hat, except for the VIPs. The World Series committee also wanted to ask two or three bigwigs from each town represented and twelve of those VIPs said yes. Then there are always some celebrity judges. This year there was a Kansas City Chief, a CNN television guy, Dwight and Simone. The committee sent out two dozen letters and this is who said yes: everyone but Dwight. The secretary remembers his personal assistant calling and asking if he could appear or something and the secretary said, how about judging? and the assistant called her back and said fine. He asked them, they didn't ask him.''

The crowd murmured and gave Stephanie some approving nods. ''Of course,'' Heaven added, ''he is going into the barbeque business big time. If he had even half a brain, he'd know this would be a good place to look for talent. Good work, though, Steph.''

Joe Long jumped up with his steno pad at the ready. Chris was on the opposite side of the room and he waved encouragement at his friend. ''Chris and I have done our phone work. Eleazar Martin needs money. His wife is divorcing him and seems to want to take him to the cleaners. That's what the treasurer of the Memphis in May contest told us. She was manning the phones at their office when I called, a volunteer position. A lovely woman, but I think she may have designs on our Aza. Kept saying what a good Christian man he was, how it's just not fair that he would have to give half of everything he had worked for all these years to his wife. Most women would think that was perfectly fair, that's why I think the treasurer has designs on Aza—she doesn't want him to be broke.

''Felicity, on the other hand, is nowhere near broke. She's loaded. I lied and told the secretary at the Charleston Barbeque Society that I was a reporter and . . .'' Joe remembered a detective was present and gave Bonnie Weber a sheepish nod, "was gathering background material on the finalists. She said Felicity was from one of the old families of Charleston, lots of money, house on the right street, all that stuff. Says Felicity has paid for things for the barbeque society, that she's a bitch but they like her. Says her girl-friend is a bit much in a small southern town but it could be worse. I did not ask what would be worse than a Grace Jones look-alike for a white rich girl's paramour." Joe looked around for approval for his restraint then continued his spiel. "Bo Morales is the darling of Amarillo. The ranchers grow special sheep for his lamb, the ladies make him calico shirts for his authentic Wild West outfits, the bankers lend him money on his little ranch when they prob-ably shouldn't. Chris got all this from Bo's niece, who just happened to answer the phone at Bo's house. She and her husband work for Bo. He raises mules and horses and they've just branched out into goats. She said Bo was going to start making goat cheese and offering cabrito, roasted young goat, at his chuck-wagon parties. She said that's how he makes most of his money, by doing these catering gigs. Michael Martin Murphy, the country singer, has this big party twice a year at his ranch and all the other ranchers like having this authentic 1890's chuck wagon do their big bashes. Bo even has a real chuck-wagon cook on his team, with a name like Tater or something."

"Buzzard, his name is Buzzard," Chris piped in.

"Lubbock, Texas, has this Cowboy Symposium every year and Bo Morales is the star. Bo wants to go into show business, be a movie star, his niece says." With that, every-one clapped and Joe sat down. Sam got up.

"Here is my diagram of the room that night. I remem-bered most of the people around the food table, H, but no one stood there as long as Murray and Simone did. Paul Taylor darted back and forth a lot. Almost everyone on the list at the bottom of the page was at the food table sometime during the night. The only person I don't remember seeing until close to the end, for Simone, I mean, was Ben Franklin.

I think I would have remembered. His outfit was very distinctive. I got a list of who RSVP'd to the World Series committee and then I added all of us and wrote everyone down. Detective, here's your copy.'' Sam had unrolled one of his masterpieces while he talked. It was detailed and color-coded. Sam should have gone to architecture school. Heaven gave him a kiss on the cheek.

''Sal, anything on Pigpen or Ben Franklin?''

Sal was the only one not sitting down. He had taken this break from cutting hair as an opportunity to clean his mirrors and had spent the last few minutes spraying glass cleaner and polishing, unlit cigar firmly in place in his mouth. ''Those two were big buddies down at the courthouse. Why, just the day before Pigpen checked out, a friend of mine saw the two of them in deep conversation. Ben Franklin is a building inspector and Pigpen was a plumber,'' Sal paused to let the import of that sink in, ''who just received a big contract to replace all the pipes in the courthouse.''

Everyone oohed and aahed over Sal's information and the way Sal could always shake the tree and come up with something. Barbara was the last team member to make her report, except for Heaven and Bonnie. She was new at this junior G-man game.

''I called my friend who's in the same chef's organization that Simone was the president of. Simone was very touchy about Dwight. She was married to a newspaper reporter when she lived in Washington, D.C. My friend didn't realize that Simone had been hitched to someone else until one night when they went out for a drink after a meeting. Simone told her about Dwight and that he had broken her heart. Dwight was just getting big at that time, about five years ago. Anyway, I guess he was performing in the Washington area and that started the conversation. Simone talked about going to his hotel, making a scene, but my friend took her home instead. Very definitely bad blood. Careerwise, I guess her California-cuisine cooking school is very popular in Paris. Last month she told my friend that she was going to write a new cookbook about something totally different, about wood-fire cooking, barbeque plus pit and fireplace cooking and tandoors in India, all that stuff.'' Barbara suddenly realized not everyone present was a trained cook. They probably didn't find this talk of tandoors as fascinating as she did. "That's all my friend could tell me.''

Heaven got up again and started her usual bussing of Sal's place, throwing empty coffee cups and napkins away. She paused with her hands full of debris. "Very interesting that Simone was going to write about forms of barbeque. That could explain why she came here, if we eliminate Dwight and revenge and all the more juicy angles. My assignment was all the leftovers. I, too, found out that Dwight and Simone were married to each other. I also talked to Paul Taylor and begged him to level with me. I went through all the weird events that he had been a part of, and he did tell me one thing I didn't know. Paul Taylor got a cut of the Pigpen sauce money because he was one of Pigpen's partners when they developed that sauce. But part of the agreement was that Paul wouldn't use the sauce in competition and didn't have access to the recipe, and he hinted that Pigpen was blackmailing him. Paul also told me someone wants to buy the recipe, which is still missing, according to Paul. He wouldn't tell me who it was that wanted to buy it. He also wouldn't tell me who their other sauce partners might be and it sounded like he was going to try to make a deal without them, whoever they are. Pigpen's bad habits seem to be spreading.''

Heaven plunged ahead, not giving anyone time to ask questions. "I thought I was so smart when I asked a friend of mine to check some phone records''—she shot a guilty glance toward Bonnie—"and he did come up with great information.'' Heaven waved around a long fax. "The only trouble is that every single one of the front-runners called Paul Taylor in the days before they arrived in Kansas City.

So did Dwight Brooks and Simone Springer. No one is eliminated.''

"Who else did they call?" Chris asked.

Heaven shook her head. "Everyone called everyone else. I guess I was hoping for a single phone call that would be like the lightbulb over the head. Felicity called Aza, Bo, Paul and Pigpen. Bo called Felicity, Aza, Paul. Aza called Bo, Felicity, Paul and Pigpen. Pigpen called Paul. Paul called Pigpen, and they didn't officially speak to each other. The only person out of this orgy of phones is Ben Franklin, but only because there was no phone listed in his name. Bonnie, I don't suppose you know how to find Ben's phone number, do you?"

Bonnie stood up and stretched her arms. "And I thought I was so smart when I went through official channels to get all these bozos' phone records. How silly of me. How could I have been so dumb? From now on I'll just call Heaven's friend and save the paperwork. I'm also going through official channels to get Ben's home number so give me another hour or so, okay? You guys are really something. I will never admit it if you found out something that I didn't know myself. My ego just won't allow it. The two things I can't figure out, you didn't mention either.''

Chris bit. "What two things?"

"Who dunnit and how does Heaven fit in?"

Chapter 27

Who dunnit and how does Heaven fit in? Who dunnit and how does Heaven fit in? The questions that Bonnie had asked rolled through Heaven's head like a mantra. Those two questions certainly caused chaos at the powwow this morning at Sal's. Everyone had started free-forming their own personal theories. Bonnie had told them all to butt out. Heaven had told them all to keep digging. Sal had told them all just to pray that this next weekend would be nice and quiet, someone would win, everyone would go home. No one liked that idea. When the contest was over, the chance of finding the killer was over too, everyone explained to Sal. So what, Sal said. It wouldn't be the first unsolved mystery in Kansas City history, or the last.

Heaven pulled in the parking lot of Kemper Arena. It was like a carnival or amusement park on a dark day. The funnel-cake wagon didn't smell like grease, the tents were empty, the streets of Barbeque Village silent. Thank goodness it wasn't dark. The powerful overhead lights of the parking lot were on and the security guards were walking the perimeter slowly. It was early evening but light was already failing. Over by the chuck wagon, Heaven saw the glow of wood embers. She waved at the guard and headed for Bo.

"Heaven, I'm so glad you were able to get away. By the way, in the confusion the other night I didn't tell you how interesting your restaurant was or how good the food was."

Heaven laughed and deposited a bottle of wine in Bo's open hands. "There's just something about a dead body that makes you forget those niceties that your mother taught you. Speaking of interesting places, I'm looking forward to learning about this chuck-wagon cooking. Walk me around this rig."

"Not until you have a glass of wine in your hand. What did you bring?"

Heaven pulled the bottle out of the sack. "A Rhône red, Vieux Telegraph. It goes great with smoky meats."

"Perfect for later, but now let's have this," Bo said as he pulled a bottle of Veuve Cliquot out of a zinc-lined tub filled with ice. He also had two beautiful flute glasses sticking out of the ice.

"I love this particular Champagne. How did you know?"

"I didn't, just followed my instincts. Most people don't know how good sparkling wines are with barbeque." Bo popped the cork and poured the wine with fluid, smooth movements.

"How long were you a waiter?" Heaven asked.

Bo smiled. "Good observation, Heaven. Three years, in Dallas. But I was a waiter only one of those years. People of Hispanic heritage usually start out washing dishes, then if you're bright, you can get the privilege of peeling onions, then maybe prep cook or busboy. I did it all."

Heaven wanted to apologize to Bo for how unfair life is. She kept her mouth shut as he started showing her all the antique gadgets on the chuck wagon.

"You know, in Texas, we have special chuck-wagon contests, where we chuck-wagon cookers just compete among ourselves. Everything on the chuck wagon has to be authentic, no imitations or modern equipment. If you have a coffee grinder on your wagon, it has to be an old one and it has to work. We dig these pits and cook our meat in big cast-iron Dutch ovens that we bury in the ashes. I usually use mesquite and oak, but since I'm in Kansas City, I thought I'd try some of your hickory and apple wood to-night.''

The wagon was fully equipped with lots of strap-ons: grease pots, a zinc-top table, tinware bowls and cups, wash-boards, a scythe. There was no foil, no plastic coolers, no electricity. Although at this World Series Bo could use any of those things legally, he wanted to win doing it the chuck-wagon way.

Heaven was totally charmed by the thought of preserving some old cooking procedures and methods. The thought of what real chuck-wagon cooks went through cooking the calf that couldn't make it to Abilene made her tired and queasy. As she asked questions about chuck-wagon history, Bo fed her. He pulled out some cowboy stew, as he called it. It was kind of an American version of cassoulet, with white beans, sausage and beef and a complex heat Heaven guessed came from dried chilis. Great flour tortillas magically appeared. Then he brought up some ribs that Heaven thought were better than any she had tasted last weekend. Next he un-buried a wild turkey stuffed with a hot sausage that wasn't chorizo but wasn't country either. Everything was delicious. Bo seemed to know what he was doing all right.

Cowboy Cassoulet

1. Oven roast 5 lbs. of trimmed beef stew meat. Sea-son with salt and pepper, 2 cinnamon sticks, a handful of garlic cloves and 2 ancho chilies soaked in warm water (use the water too). Roast at 375 degrees, 2–3 hours, until the meat is tender. Cool and refrigerate; then remove the fat that has con-gealed on the top.
2. Soak and cook 2 lbs. dried northern beans, adding salt after the beans are tender. Cool the beans by surrounding the pot with an ice-water bath in the

sink or transferring the hot beans into shallow plastic containers. Beans are easily soured, so it is important to not put them in the refrigerator hot. It will take too long for the middle of the pot to cool.

3. 3 lbs. hot or mild Italian sausage or a combination of the two. Prick the sausage with a fork on both sides. Roast 25 minutes at 375 degrees. Cool the sausage and cut into three-inch chunks.

4. Finely dice 2–3 onions, 4 peeled carrots, and 6 celery stalks. Saute until onions are clear. In a large ovenproof roasting pan, combine the defatted beef, the beans, sausage and the vegetables. Add 1 large can of tomatoes, 2 more ancho chilies that have been soaked in warm water, and enough chicken stock to make the whole mixture very wet. Do not combine until right before you bake or the beans will absorb the moisture and the dish will be dry. Top the mixture with toasted bread crumbs and bake at 350 degrees until the sides are bubbling, the crumbs have browned and formed a crust, and the middle of the casserole is hot.

"Where'd you get that wild turkey?" Heaven asked.

"I had it sent from a wild-game farm that's right down the road from my little place. I'm going to cook one for the competition this weekend so you see, you've done me a favor by allowing me to experiment on you."

"You are very gallant, a corny word I know, but it describes you. How did you get so wise?" Heaven knew this could be construed as flirting but she couldn't help herself.

"Through suffering, of course," Bo said lightly. He didn't want to finish the conversation, so he got up to put on the coffee pot. Eggshells were involved in the coffee making. Heaven wanted to know more about his suffering but she didn't have the strength to be pushy tonight. There's also the slightest chance that he's the killer, she thought, and if I make him think unpleasant thoughts he may take it out on me.

Heaven drank her coffee as fast as she could. She needed to get home before she forgot who she was and crawled in the chuck wagon with Bo Morales. She knew that Bo was really staying at the Ritz-Carlton but not going to the Ritz with Bo wasn't half as romantic as not getting in the chuck wagon with him.

"A penny for your thoughts," Bo said wistfully.

"No way. I'll tell you what I should have been thinking instead. I should have been thinking of all that I've learned tonight and all the wonderful food you made. You're a good cook, Bo. I wish you good luck this weekend. Who do you think is the team to beat?"

Bo kissed her hand. "The team I don't know is always the most dangerous team. Everyone was fooled by Ben Franklin, Heaven. We won't make that mistake again this weekend."

"We?" Heaven let her eyebrows arch high into the *I Love Lucy* curve. She wanted to tell Bo that Ben wasn't competition in the way they thought, but she didn't.

Bo wasn't the least bit flustered by her questioning expression. "I know Aza and Felicity were just as surprised by Ben as I was. Not that we can prevent the judges from voting for him. But we just weren't expecting him, that's what I'm trying to say. And I'm also trying to tell you what a wonderful evening I've had with you. I hope it is the first of many evenings we spend together in our lives."

Heaven fell into her bad southern accent. "Why Mr. More-rail-lays. How you do go on." She stepped up close and kissed Bo with at least as much relish as Felicity had kissed her earlier in the day. He pulled her tighter but she knew she had a one-kiss limit. She spun free with a laugh and never looked back as she hightailed it for the car. "I'm outta here. See you tomorrow," she yelled over her shoulder.

The sound of Bo's laughter and his "Adios, Heaven," were almost irresistible.

As she made her way to Fifth Street in the van, Heaven wondered if it was too late to call Bonnie Weber.

Chapter 28

She knew everyone would be mad at her. She had intruded into the barbeque world. Now she was changing things. But after her conversation with several members of the World Series committee this morning she had a hunch they were going to take her suggestion. It actually made perfect sense in light of the ecumenical nature of the contest.

Heaven parked near Latte Land on the stylish Country Club Plaza. Bonnie Weber was sitting in the window. She looked up and gave her friend a little smile. Bonnie looked tired and worried. Heaven ordered her double latte and sat down.

"You look like shit."

Bonnie barely fought back. "My husband said the same thing. I haven't been sleeping very well. I can't help thinking that whoever is doing this can just have their way with us this weekend. I can't stop them, I'll confess."

"Because you don't know who or why, really. Bonnie, I wish I could say I have it all figured out but I don't. But I need to tell you what I've done."

"You're scaring me."

"Heaven, your latte is ready," the barista yelled. Heaven went over to the counter and got her brew, then returned to the counter beside Bonnie. "I asked the committee to change the way that the contest is scored. And I did that because I have reason to believe that the scores were rigged somewhat last weekend.''

''How?''

''Which how?''

Bonnie wanted to wring Heaven's neck. ''How will they change the scoring? How was it rigged? How do you know about the rigging?''

Heaven selected the easiest how. ''The way the contest was scored last week was the Kansas City way. The teams get their first numbers when they enter. They get containers for their entries and these containers have numbers on them. The numbers are covered up with a second set of numbers. And someone from the Barbeque Guild lines up all those numbers with the scanner sheets from the scoring. If someone wanted to cheat, the person who lines up all these numbers with the scores with the team names would be capable of doing so. It's easy to change things on a computer, we all know that. So . . .''

Bonnie cut in. ''And you think someone cheated last weekend because . . . ?''

''Because I borrowed some of the scoring sheets from last weekend.''

''Borrowed?''

''Don't make me lie to you. Just know that there is a perfect alternative scoring method.''

''And what is that?''

''The ticket method. Each entry container has a torn ticket taped on the top of the box. The numbers are covered during judging but there are no second sets of numbers. The team is responsible for keeping their half of the tickets. When they announce the winners, they announce numbers: fourth place, number three-twenty-two. The teams have to look at their tickets and then they go up and say who they are, The Rib Rustlers or whoever. Until then, the committee members don't have a clue who won either.''

''When they give out the containers, they don't write down who they give the tickets to?''

Heaven shook her head. "No. It is chancy because of that. What if you lost your half of the tickets for your teams? You have to be careful. But they use this method in Texas all the time and everyone manages to keep hold of their stubs. It's just like the lottery. Everyone knows they have to have their lottery ticket to claim victory."

"Are you going to tell me what sent you over the edge on this issue?"

"I wish there was one thing I could tell you. Last night I spent some time with Bo Morales and he used the term 'we.' "

Bonnie hid her eyes with her hands. "And?"

"And I got this idea that maybe the top contenders were in cahoots with Paul Taylor."

"To do what? Hand the grand prize over to Ben Franklin? I understand that your illegally obtained phone records"— Bonnie paused and gave Heaven a stern look—"do show activity between all those parties, but why would they fix the fight against themselves?"

"Well, I was wrong so don't worry about it. Maybe Ben paid Paul more than the others did. Maybe the whole thing got screwed up with Pigpen's murder."

"And how does Simone fit in?" Bonnie was rustling through her legal pads.

"Bonnie, I don't have a clue. Now that we know she was married to Dwight Brooks, maybe it had something to do with him. I don't have any of the answers, but it just makes more sense to use another scoring method this week. And the committee agreed with me. After all, they're using another judging method so why not change it all?"

"What's the judging method?"

"A three-tiered system, semifinals and finals after the initial judging. Each category also gets its own set of judges this week. The idea is to let as many people as possible taste each team's product, so six people won't decide your fate. It takes more time. First round, they will score everyone's ribs and the lowest-scoring twenty teams will be eliminated.

Then the rib judges split up into semifinal and final. One team of rib judges will do the semifinals blind tasting. They will eliminate down to twenty for the rib finals. This means the finalists will have been tasted by three judging teams. Also this week the on-site judging will add another score to the final totals. There will be another set of judges for that. I'm on that team this week.''

Bonnie Weber got up from her stool and stretched. ''What did you tell the committee?''

''Just that there was no reason to leave room for criticism when there was another method that everyone could agree upon. I said that Paul Taylor knew many of the participants and I knew they didn't want anyone to call foul ball because of that. They probed around to try to get me to say there was more to it. I don't know what I'm doing, Bonnie. This insanity was caused by looking at those phone records and hearing Bo say 'we' and then there are these rigged scores in favor of Ben Franklin, for God's sake. Also Paul tells me someone, he won't say who, is still bidding for the secret sauce. I suspect Dwight Brooks on that one. He needs good recipes from all around the country for his concept. Why wouldn't he come here to shop? And maybe Simone was trying to prevent him from getting the choice sauce recipes or maybe she wanted them for herself since she was working on a wood-fire cookbook. It kills me I can't talk to Pigpen and Simone about this.''

''Heaven, don't say 'kills me,' especially in connection with those two.''

''Oops. Please don't put me back on the suspect list for that one.''

''Heaven, what makes you think you ever left the suspect list? The facts are you found the first victim and provided the means for the second. Don't forget that I don't get to eliminate my friends and don't forget that the prosecutor's office has some say in this.''

Heaven got up and waved as she headed for the door. ''I think I should quit while I'm ahead.''

Hours later, as she fileted salmon, Heaven sighed and looked back on her morning conversation with Bonnie. The detective was trying to warn her that she was looking good as the perp in these cases. The only way to eliminate herself as prime suspect was to find the real killer.

Someone yelled from the front of the house, "Heaven, it's Stephanie on line three." Heaven grabbed the phone.

"Can you pick me up?" Stephanie asked.

"Of course. Barbara's guys are going down around four with Barbara's rig. They're going to start making camp. I told her we'd be there at six. Barbara won't be down until tomorrow morning. She has a big Italian rehearsal dinner at the restaurant. Meridith and Sally Jo will be down for a couple of hours, but we really don't need them if the camp is set up for us."

"Thank God we didn't start this barbeque stuff when we were young and poor instead of now when we have access to a staff," Stephanie sniffed. "Can you imagine doing all that physical labor yourself?"

"I'll see you soon," Heaven said as way of good-bye. She hung up the wall phone and turned around only to be nose to nose with Ben Franklin. Today's outfit was an Air Force surplus jumpsuit that Ben had been having barbeque teams autograph. It was covered with colorful mottos. Ben was colorful himself, red-faced and hoppin' mad by the flash in his eyes.

"Who told you to butt in, missy?"

"Ben, how about just backing up a little, give me a little breathing room, okay?" Heaven immediately regretted using the phrase "breathing room" but she had done it, she couldn't change it now without making an obvious allusion to Simone's death. It worked. Ben leaned back ever so slightly and Heaven stepped around him. "What's the problem, Ben?"

"You sticking your nose in this judging business, that's the problem. You're not on the dadblame committee or on a team so what do you care how the dadblame contest is scored?''

"Ben, what do you care? The IBCA method is just as good as the Kansas City method. If you're not cheating, then . . .''

Ben Franklin stamped his foot. "I'm not cheating and now everyone will think I am. It looks like no one could believe ol' Ben Franklin and pitiful little Mickey could possibly be in first place legit. No, they'd have to've cheated. Is that what you thought, missy?''

"Not at all. I'm curious, Ben. Where did you hear that it was my idea to go to another kind of scoring this week? I merely had a suggestion. No one had to listen to me. And I wanted us, Kansas City and the guild, to be beyond reproach. This way we've used every different way to judge and score. What's the matter with that?''

"It makes me look bad, that's what's the matter. And I heard it from Paul Taylor, that's who. He's ticked off too.''

"I bet he is.'' Heaven blanched inwardly at the thought. Why did the committee have to tell everyone it was her idea to change the scoring? If she had been shot at last week, before she stuck her nose in this mess, what would happen now? "Ben, this is personal, exactly. Good luck to you this weekend. I hope you win lots of money, or get whatever you're after. I'm sure you deserve to be in first place and no one suggested we start over from scratch, that you lose your points from last week. I could see you having a gripe if that had been the case. But, Ben, you're still on top. What's your real problem?''

"My good name, that's what.''

"Well, Ben, I can't help it if you're not the most popular guy on the barbeque contest circuit. Take a class in how to make friends. Now that you've given me a piece of your mind, do you think we can both go our separate ways?''

"Just stay out of my way this weekend, missy. I'm warning you.'' With that dramatic garnish to their little talk, Ben Franklin swept out of the kitchen via the door to the alley.

The kitchen crew had been watching this whole scene, trying to catch Heaven's eye now and then. Brian Hoffman was impressed. "Wow, like an evil dude comes in and threatens you, man. We heard him, man, in case, you know, something really happens."

Heaven threw her hair over to the side of her head so her new scar could show. Yesterday, she had gone over to the medical center and had the stitches removed. "Brian, something has already happened, as you can see by this rather unattractive gash on my head. I am not looking forward to what might constitute 'something really happening' in your mind. Please don't get ready for testifying in court just yet. But I am glad you all were here"—she looked over at Robbie and Pauline—"because I think he might have smacked me if we'd been alone. I'm going to make my rounds now, talk to the front of the house, get ready to leave. I'm spending the night out at Barbeque Village. It's my turn to cook for the Que Queens."

Brian's eyes widened again. "You're going to spend the night where the dude is? Whoa."

"Thank you so much for that vote of confidence," Heaven joked. The look on Pauline's face told Heaven she was worried too. "I'll be safe and sound in a big Winnebago thing. It's got everything home has. No problem."

Then why did Heaven feel that sinking feeling again?

Chapter 29

Stephanie and Heaven were putting their feet up, relaxing and drinking some wine, a Calera Pinot Noir. The young men who worked for Barbara Carollo had done all the hard work. They had positioned the travel vehicle, the smoker and the tents. Everything was unloaded and the spatulas were lined up next to the tongs. Heaven had started the fire that was now burning down. Stephanie had gone in to the cooks' meeting, not because they were required to, but to see what they would say about the change in scoring methods. She had just returned and filled her glass.

"So, no one mentioned your name," Stephanie reported smugly.

"Thank goodness," Heaven said with a big sigh. She had been holding that thought and her breath the whole time Stephanie had been inside.

"They said how they were trying to use all the various scoring and judging methods from different parts of the country. Last week it was one way, this week another. No one was shocked. No one asked why. Paul and Ben Franklin kept their mouths shut. Everyone got a sheet with the schedule for judging tomorrow and also the time of the on-site judging. They also explained how there was going to be three-tiered judging and ticket identification. Texas teams were explaining the ticket method to their neighbors. It couldn't have gone smoother. I don't think we'll get fire-bombed tonight, H.''

"Now all we have to do is make the best ribs and pork shoulder we've ever made. I intend for us to win this silly contest again tomorrow. I'm not even going to worry about the brisket."

Stephanie laughed. "Good, because neither one of us can cook brisket for shit. Mine is always a stringy mess."

"Brisket is not my idea of a good cut of meat. I've never understood why people like it. My mom used the old dry onion soup and Worcestershire sauce method on the farm. I still think that's the way to go."

"Heaven Lee, you should be ashamed. You have cooked with some of the best chefs in the world. You yourself are famous for your innovative turns and twists. And you would cook a brisket with dry onion soup? Naughty girl."

Mrs. O'Malley's Brisket

1 whole or half beef brisket
1 or 2 boxes dry onion soup mix
Worcestershire sauce

On the fat side of the brisket, make a crisscross pattern with a knife. Now take the dry onion soup mix and smoosh it down in the brisket. The scoring will help keep it in place. Wet the whole thing with the sauce. Roast for 30 minutes at 400 degrees. Reduce heat to 250 degrees, cover the meat with foil and bake for hours, until the meat is fork tender. This will take 2–5 hours, depending on the size of the brisket. Throw a cup of water or red wine on once in a while.

Heaven raised her glass in mock salute. "And proud of it. Shall we go over to the party? It's at the K.C. Masterpiece Barbeque Sauce tent tonight. We'll have to take turns, of course. I'm sure that my new popularity with some members of the barbeque community should be translated into 'never leave your meat unattended.' I can just see someone pouring a ton of Tabasco on the pork or something.''

''Or something. I can see that nasty Ben Franklin committing sabotage all right. I wish you hadn't told me about his scene at the cafe. *And* I wish you hadn't gone on that search-and-steal mission without me. Why would Paul help Ben? Nobody likes Ben.''

''The scene at the cafe is probably an example of why Ben isn't that popular. But think of it this way, it could have been worse. It could have been Pigpen yelling and getting in my face.''

''You know, Heaven, I was just thinking about old Pigpen. How I'm gonna miss him in a twisted kind of a way.'' Stephanie was applying eyeliner as she spoke. ''The Battle of the Sexes would never have happened without him.''

Heaven watched as Stephanie brought out the mascara wand. ''I'm sure we would have come up with another way to make money for charity, Steph. Now that you've freshened your makeup, as they used to say, why don't you take that beautiful face and go to the party with it?''

Stephanie smiled at her image in the makeup mirror she had pulled out of her overnight bag earlier. ''I do good work. If I can make a plate of sausages look appealing, I can make anything look appealing. I'll check out the scene. Be back in a while.''

Because the Que Queens were not an official contest team, Heaven had kept her ribs in a cooler inside the RV. Now she took them out and started the task of removing the membrane that holds a slab of ribs together. Restaurants couldn't afford the labor hours to remove this membrane, but cooking contestants often took the time to do so. The Queens also used back ribs when they cooked, the part of the ribs located on the loin of a pig. The less expensive spareribs came from the side.

Pulling membrane was relaxing, mindless work, and Heaven was enjoying herself. Barbeque Village was alive with activity. The excitement level was higher than it had been the week before. There were more cookers around too because there were more side activities this weekend.

Last weekend the Battle of the Sexes had been the only cooking side activity. There had been those darling clog dancers and the bands but no one else competing in cooking events. This weekend there was a backyard barbeque contest for backyard cookers who would come and set up early Saturday morning. There was also an open sausage competition sponsored by Farmland Pork Products, a chili cook-off and a steak grilling competition. By tomorrow morning, there would be close to three hundred teams spread out on the parking lots around Kemper Arena, all busy doing something.

The chili cookers were the wildest. They already had their territory staked out, and campers and RVs were pouring in. Making chili didn't really require an overnight stay, but it wouldn't be a party if you just moseyed in on a Saturday afternoon with a pot of beans and meat. No, the chili folks came early and stayed late. They brought their grills as well as propane burners, grilling burgers and bratwursts the night before a competition. Some had campfire tripods with big hanging cast-iron kettles for their concoctions. Some had metal stands and propane tanks like the ones they used in New Orleans to cook crayfish and turkeys outdoors.

In New Orleans, they put a heavy-duty stockpot on top of the stand and, for special occasions, boiled whole turkeys in oil. Heaven had been amazed the first time she tasted one of these creations. The hot oil seared the turkey and it was moist and flavorful, not greasy as she had expected. By the smells in the air, someone was boiling turkeys tonight, along with grilling steaks and burgers and maybe something spicy like jerk pork. Heaven could pick up the aroma of cayenne and cumin in the October air.

As Heaven was humming and skinning her ribs, Aza Martin came down the street. "Heaven, I've got some gumbo here that should put Emeril to shame." Emeril was a well-known chef in New Orleans and this was Aza's way of saying the gumbo should be good.

"Perfect timing. I'm starved," Heaven said as she dipped her hands in a bleach and water solution and gave her nails a whisk with a nail brush. In Heaven's experience barbeque cookers were more germ conscious than most food professionals who cooked indoors. She had become more bacteria aware and used bleach and water solution all the time at the cafe.

"Aza, did you bring this with you from Memphis, honey?" Heaven stuck her nose in the pail of gumbo and inhaled. "That's the cayenne I smelled on the air. What sausage?"

"Crayfish boudin and no, this is no Memphis gumbo. These old boys from Baton Rouge are camping next to me. They made gumbo tonight and I'll make breakfast tomorrow. Of course, they cooked for an army. So, Heaven, I hear you got through the week without another fatality. Good work."

Heaven slammed a beer in front of Aza with mock anger. "Give me a break, will ya? Making it without a murder from Monday to Friday is hardly an accomplishment to brag about. The worst part is that the police don't seem to have a suspect that they can really settle down on."

Aza looked up with what Heaven thought was relief on his face. "That so? Well, maybe Simone and Pigpen don't have nothin' to do with each other. Maybe neither of them dying has anything to do with the contest. Could be."

Heaven sat down near Aza and dug into the pot of soup. "Well, Pigpen couldn't be a wonderful guy in his real life, oops, couldn't have been. He took entirely too much glee in the little things, like ridicule and lording it over you when he won. The plumbers of Kansas City must be celebrating this week."

"I know the cookers are," Aza said with a chuckle. He caught himself and tried to erase the grin from his face.

"Yoo-hoo, you two. What's cookin' over here?" Stephanie was returning from the party with an entourage. Heaven spotted Alice Aron, Felicity June Morgan, Felicity's girlfriend and several others. Felicity had a bottle of champagne in her hand and someone popped the cork. All of a sudden it was a party. In twenty minutes dozens of cookers and their families were milling around, beers in hand. Someone had a CD of old R&B and before they knew what hit them, they were dancing in the streets to James Brown funk. The next thing Heaven knew it was almost midnight. Dr. Rich Davis, the founder of K.C. Masterpiece Barbeque Sauce, came over to shake Heaven's hand.

"Well, you picked right up where the official function left off, didn't you. They don't call you all the Queens for nothing," Dr. Davis joked.

Felicity slunk up to Heaven and the doctor, throwing one arm around each of them. "In case you hadn't noticed, Doc, this whole contest is full of royal attitude. There are more queens here, male and female, than in Europe."

Heaven slipped out of Felicity's grasp but not until she pinched Felicity's bottom. "See what you started, Rich. Now I'm going to have to run everyone off." Heaven yelled, "Everybody, it's time to put your meat on the fire. Go to work so I can go to work."

Reluctantly, the groups went back to their own camps, to start their meat, drink more beer and tell more lies.

The younger men and women were not the least bit ready to go to sleep. Indeed, young women in Kansas City had been known to come out to the barbeque contest after the bars closed to be in on the excitement and adventure. The chilly fall nights, the smell of hardwood fires, and the cute, young, male participants all were big draws. Music drifted from every direction. Heaven could pick out reggae, cowboy and Tony Bennett now that she had turned off her own beloved Aretha. As she and Stephanie spiced up the pork shoulder and brisket, they told each other tales of the night, giggling and talking too much.

"H, this is more fun than sex," Stephanie said. "I haven't

even checked my makeup for hours, that's how much fun I've been having.''

"I noticed. I didn't know you actually had pale lips like the rest of us. You ate a huge Italian sausage sandwich with onions and peppers without reapplying. I'm so glad you brought that crew back with you. We had the best party on the block, that's for sure.'' Heaven yawned. "Now I'm beat. We have two hours until the fire will need a couple of logs.''

"And the meat will need to be moved,'' Stephanie said sleepily. She opened the door of the RV. "Our suite awaits, sweetie.''

"I'll take the lower bunk and get up for the first go round.'' Heaven dug around in her bag for the travel alarm. She set it and closed her eyes. Sleep came fast.

The beeping noise interrupted Heaven's slumber much too soon. As she tried to turn over and go back to the dream state, Heaven realized that the beeping wasn't her familiar alarm sound. She shook herself free from sleep and realized a different alarm was going off, a loud insistent one. Smoke? No, it wasn't smoky in here. As she sat on the side of the bed she smelled the overpowering smell of gas. The blinking box near the door was ringing. She jumped up and shook Stephanie, who was trying to get up at that very moment. "Shit, it smells like . . .''

"Gas. Let's get out of here fast,'' Heaven said as she helped her friend jump down from the top bunk. They opened the door of the RV and let the cool night air hit their lungs. The alarm was even louder outside. People were running from all directions. As the two women staggered out, Bo Morales came into their camp at a gallop. He grabbed Heaven and Stephanie.

Heaven looked at Bo. "Is it going to blow up? Do we need to take cover?''

Bo looked in the open door. "That's your LP detector. Let's just disconnect this propane tank first.'' Bo worked fast and as the other cookers came in the camp and talked with Bo, Heaven could see concern in their faces. Bo and a couple of others went into the RV and came out with grim looks.

Bo seemed to be elected to explain. "Heaven, these RVs have two power sources, a generator and propane. The generator is responsible for the air conditioning, lights, outlet electricity, sometimes the refrigerator. It, the generator, is fed by a special line from the gas tank. The propane tank runs the hot-water heater, furnace, stove and, in this case, the refrigerator. Someone pulled the connection between the refrigerator and the propane line loose. Then just to be sure you'd get a snoot full of gas, they turned on the stove burners and blew out the pilot light. You must have fallen right asleep, then the LP detector alarm went off."

Heaven looked at her watch. It was only twelve-forty. They had only been in bed thirty minutes max. "Bo, you know a lot about RVs for a guy who travels in a chuck wagon." She realized immediately how suspicious she sounded, not that she didn't have plenty of reason for suspicion. Bo had been the first person on the scene, even though his rig was a couple blocks away. Maybe she should try being cool for a change.

"Heaven, I don't travel around the country behind a mule team, and even if I did, I know a few people who own these newfangled machines." Bo's voice was dripping with sarcasm.

"Bo, I'm sorry. You came over here and saved us and I practically accuse you of . . . of saving us too good. I'm kind of mixed up. I went to sleep just a few minutes ago and then the loud noise and the gas . . ."

Bo took Heaven's arm and led her to a chair. Someone had already sat Stephanie down and handed her a cup of coffee. She looked up bleakly. "H, will you check the fire? I feel sick, what with the gas smell and all the beer and wine I drank. I hope we haven't ruined Barbara's house."

"Of course I'll check the fire. I know it needs a log or two. And Barbara's house, as you call it, is fine. We didn't break anything. It can all be hooked up again in the morning. But, Steph, we have to go back in there and try to sleep. The door's been open for a while. I'm sure it's aired out and we'll be fine.''

As Heaven tended the fire and moved the briskets and pork shoulders, Bo Morales knelt down beside Stephanie. He kissed her hand. ''You are both welcome to come and sleep at my camp. The boys have a tent and they can just sleep in the truck.''

Stephanie shook her head. ''No way. Whoever did this didn't want to knock us off. They must have known there was a liquid-propane detector in the RV and it would go off. If they had really wanted to kill us, they could've taken the batteries out of the detector since they had time to disconnect tubes and carry on. They've made their point. I'm sure we'll be fine. We've got cooking to do.''

Bo stood up and gave both women the movie-star smile. ''Then maybe I should stay here with you two.''

The crowd of cookers started hooting and laughing, moving back toward their own camps.

''You old dog.''

''That's our cue to go home.''

''Heaven, you call us if you need us.''

''Bo, did you plan this thing to get in bed with these girls?''

As the campsite cleared out, Bo moved Heaven's hair off her forehead and kissed her scar. She melted but did not move or grab his hand and drag him into the RV. She could still remember the kiss of last night all too well. And she did love Hank, really.

''Bo, thanks. See you in the morning.''

Heaven and Stephanie hugged Bo on their way to the motor home. When they were inside, Stephanie whined. ''H, can I sleep with you? I sounded real butch out there a minute ago but I want to go home in the worst way. I wouldn't leave you here by yourself for the world, of course. But I want to. So, can we make spoons?''

Heaven had to laugh. Her mother used to use that term

for when you sleep back side to front side and fit in the crooks of the other person's body. "You come right here beside me. I'm setting the alarm for two hours from now. We are not going to cry like babies. We are not going to call Barbara or Meridith and make them come down here in the middle of the night. We are going to get through this. Now close your eyes."

They both closed their eyes tight. They were being brave for each other.

Chapter 30

To say the day started early was an understatement. The night just never ended. The assembly line of time was relentless; there was no sleep break in the Alpha level. The ribs went on the smoker at five. Now it was seven and their heady smell, pungent from the new dry rub, mingled with the fully mature aromas of the brisket and the pork shoulder.

The same radio station that sponsored the Battle of the Sexes broadcast live from the contest hosted a team breakfast this Saturday. Stephanie had gone over and loaded up on breakfast burritos and muffins and some very unappetizing fruit. She and Heaven were eating and telling the other Queens about their wild night. Barbara and Sally Jo and Meridith were all present and accounted for. Barbara was reconnecting her propane line.

Heaven was starting to take these brushes with death personally. "I have a theory. Paul Taylor doesn't like me. Whaddaya think?"

Sally Jo looked puzzled. "Now, did I miss something? I don't remember Paul being one of the characters in last night's tale. But Aza and Felicity and Bo were all here at some time and could have tampered with your gas line."

Heaven wasn't going to let a little thing like the facts deter her. "Why would they want to? I'm not another contestant. My judging alone couldn't decide anything. I'm insignificant in their lives. But I think Paul Taylor is convinced I have the Pigpen sauce recipe in my possession. Oh, and I know he knows I got them to change the scoring rules for this weekend. I'm sure he's pissed about that. He practically sent Ben Franklin over to bite me.''

Stephanie was adding an apple log to the fire. She hadn't missed out on Heaven's faulty logic so she hollered across the camp. "First of all, you better fill everyone in on the Ben Franklin visit. And your little raid of the guild office. That was clear back Thursday and Friday. So much has happened since then. Then, allow me to point out that your changing the scoring system might make a difference to Aza or Felicity or Bo, don't you think?''

Meridith jumped in. "But if Ben Franklin is in first place, how would this work?"

Heaven was glad to see someone else go down that path. "Exactly. I would think they would be thrilled to see a change that might make the playing field more equal. That is, if Paul Taylor is cheating. Or was cheating. And the very fact that we didn't see Paul last night is suspicious. Almost everyone else showed up for ten minutes at least. Even Dr. Davis, who was hosting his own party, came over. Where was Paul Taylor?''

A female voice boomed from down the pathway. "In the hospital with severe gastric distress. Stomach pains.'' It was Detective Bonnie Weber. "I hear I missed the excitement last night. Someone tried to give you two a big headache?'' Bonnie plopped down at the table and yelled, "Any coffee?'' Barbara came out of the RV with a pot in her hand. She poured a cup for the detective and went round the group.

"How did you find out so soon?'' Heaven asked Bonnie. It was barely eight on a Saturday morning. Everyone knew it took longer to process information on weekends.

"I have developed a few information pipelines in this barbeque world. After all, I've been hanging around it for a week and a half now.''

"So, what's the matter with Paul?" everyone asked more or less at the same time.

"I called his house about an hour ago to ask him about your mishap. One of his kids answered the phone and said that mom had taken dad to the emergency room sometime in the night. They kept him a few hours to make sure he wasn't having a heart attack, the kid said. I'm not sure what the stomach pains had to do with the heart attack. But the kid said his dad should be home this morning sometime. Maybe someone is out to scare both you and Paul, Heaven?" Bonnie had a maddening habit of finding another way to look at things. It was one of the reasons she solved most of her cases.

Heaven threw up her hands. "Well, I'm scared. They can quit now."

Bonnie stood up. "Just try, and I know this is asking a lot, to keep out of trouble today, Heaven. Are you going to go to the restaurant?"

"No," Heaven said. "Brian is covering my shifts this weekend. I'm here for the duration. We have another Battle of the Sexes and I'm also judging the booth decor today."

Stephanie perked up. She had been dragging around all morning but the word "decor" made her come alive. "By the way, wasn't Joe coming down here to help me with our crown?"

"And here we are." It was Chris Snyder and Joe Long, carrying cutout pieces of foamcore and a tool box. "Have glitter, will travel."

Joe Long had a glue gun in one hand and a saw in the other. "Or, I prefer to say, here come the queens with the crown."

The Que Queens had been planning a giant foamcore crown that would sit on top of the RV. The World Series of Barbeque had been the perfect reason to spring for the supplies. Joe had been commissioned to make the crown. Joe made props for local theaters and knew how to make things glitter like gold when they were actually cardboard.

He had chosen the Cinderella-style crown as opposed to the tiara style. The crown was in sections and just needed to be put together, and, of course, have more glitter applied when it was in place. Stephanie climbed up on top of the motor home with the guys and soon their whoops could be heard all around the village. The tips of the crown were the full eight feet of a foamcore section and the crown stuck out three or four feet on both sides of the RV. It was going to be an imposing prop. Even though the Queens couldn't win a cash prize for their crown, it would be a traffic stopper.

When they competed, they were sometimes in the parking lots of large suburban supermarkets, where they caught shoppers coming out of the store and it was easy to get a donation of canned goods or dried pasta or staples. They raised most of the money and food for the Food Bank out in these parking lots so the crown would bring lots of attention to their cause.

Today, at the World Series of Barbeque, the crown would have serious competition for the most outrageous gimmick. All over the camp, saws and glue guns were hard at work. Pigs and cows made of every conceivable material were being erected. Bales of hay and pumpkins and other fall objects were being moved in by the truckload.

"This place looks like the reunion of department-store display managers. Jesus Christ," Bonnie Weber said with some amount of disgust. "I'm going to go throw my weight around and try to stop a killer. Heaven try to stay in crowds, please. Don't let anyone single you out."

"That shouldn't be a problem," Heaven said "*I'm* going to throw myself into my work."

Heaven wasn't alone. All the teams were getting serious.

Bo Morales was spritzing his wild turkey.

Felicity Morgan was adding the final touches to her mustard sauce.

Aza Martin was checking his ribs.

Over in the corner, Ben Franklin and Mickey had their heads buried in the trunk of the old Cadillac. They had a huge plastic vat into which they were pouring various liquids. If anyone came near the wok tower or the car, Mickey would take their hand and lead them away.

Activities for the spectators started at about ten in the morning. This weekend, a tractor company had some kind of a mini-tractor pull arranged for children. The kids raced on small, green John Deeres that had weights added to create a load on the back. A large crowd of parents had formed around this attraction. They were coaching their offspring along with cheers and driving tips.

On the big stage, the authentic chuck-wagon cook, Buzzard, who was a member of Bo Morales's cooking team, was telling a cowboy story and reciting a cowboy poem, not at the same time, of course. At the Lubbock Cowboy Symposium, he had won first place in poetry.

A huge tent held sauces for sale. Every year at the American Royal Barbeque, every team donated a case of its sauce for the sauce sale. Proceeds went to the Food Bank. The World Series had adopted the practice in its first year, with the proceeds going to the Nashville Food Bank. The sauce sale had been so popular that this year the sauce committee had asked for three cases from each contestant, one donated and the other two sold at the wholesale rate. Last year, barbeque lovers had started a trend by buying one bottle of sauce from each contestant in the World Series. Those folks were back and they brought their friends this year. People were loading up dollies with cases of bottles and recommending sauces to the general public. There was also a salsa contest, a people's choice contest very similar to the Battle of the Sexes. Contestgoers paid a dollar to vote on their favorite salsa and the money went to feed hungry people. A local Mexican restaurant, which had a burrito truck parked at the contest to sell Mexican food, had donated chips to the salsa tasting.

Heaven was dipping ribs in sauce when she saw a familiar vehicle pull up on the opposite side of the stage, in the Male Chauvinist Pigs' team area. She noticed it because it was late in the morning for anyone to be driving into the area. Most cars had been parked at the campsites or over in the team parking lots since the night before. When she heard a car pulling up this late, Heaven was ready to make a crack about the men's team sneaking in some store-bought ribs from Arthur Bryant's or Gate's. Then she looked up.

It was a black Blazer and Heaven just knew it was the car that had chased her last week. She was frozen to the spot. Of course, there were hundreds of people milling around between her and that car. Nothing bad could possibly happen now, but Heaven felt a rush of adrenaline anyway. She could hardly wait to see who got out of it. She would find Bonnie Weber and drag her over there to question the criminal. She would swear that it was the car that had attacked her. Then the car door opened and Heaven almost fainted.

The person hopping out of the car, shaking hands all around, giving greetings to one and all was not some frightening gangster type. It was not Aza, Felicity or Bo. It wasn't even Paul Taylor or Ben Franklin. It was Cork Stuecheck. Cork, who just the other day had told Heaven how he would never cook in a contest again. Cork, who had fixed her lunch, who she had confided in. Heaven dropped the ribs in the sauce vat. She had to go in up to her elbows to fish them out.

A voice chimed, "Heaven, how are you, my dear?" It was a whole troop of volunteers from the Food Bank. They swarmed over the Queens' campsite, oohed and aahed over the big crown and went over to set up the table where people paid to vote in the Battle of the Sexes. They had several large plastic trash cans that were used for cans and other grocery donations.

It was time to get on the tiaras and the royal sashes. The Queens had separated their ribs, pulled their pork and sliced their brisket. The huge crown was sparkling and glittering overhead, swaying rather grandly in the autumn breeze. Heaven moved as if in a dream. She could hardly wait to confront Cork. The two teams usually milled around on either side of the Food Bank table, exhorting the crowd to vote for them. They put out their wares, one meat category at a time. If they had put out all three meats at once, the contest would have been over in twenty minutes. There were two trays of meat on the Food Bank table, along with a stack of Battle of the Sexes ballots. Participants paid their two bucks and picked up a ballot and a sample from each tray. The trays had numbers on them and the Food Bank volunteers knew who was who. This contest was a very casual version of the real thing going on around it.

When the men's team made its way over to the voting area, Cork Stuecheck was leading the way. "Heaven, how nice to see you again so soon."

Heaven attempted to smile but she failed. She had been trying to remember everything she had blabbed last week when she thought Cork was an innocent retiree. She wondered if anything he had said to her was the truth. She wondered hopefully if she was wrong about the Blazer.

"Cork, this is a surprise. What brings you back to the scene of the crime? I mean, not a real crime, just back to your old stomping grounds. Or something." Someone needs to stop me, Heaven thought. I'm making a fool out of myself. Again.

Cork laughed. "This is a classic example of never say never. Here you and I talk and I tell you how I just can't imagine ever being in a barbeque contest again. But today Paul Taylor's wife called me and said Paul had a scare last night. I guess she had to take him to the emergency room. She asked me if I'd take over this little charity contest. Of course, they already had everything on the fire. I didn't get here until six or seven this morning."

Heaven realized that she hadn't seen Cork until almost noon. He must have just moved his car around for some reason. Maybe he'd gone to get something. What? And how early did Mrs. Taylor call Cork? Didn't Bonnie say she'd called Paul about seven and they were still at the hospital?

So what did Paul's wife do, call in the middle of the night from the hospital?

"Well, this must be a real head trip for you," Heaven said as she guided Cork around to the front of the contest area. She pointed up at the crown like she was spotting Mt. Rushmore for the first time. "Have you looked around at all the excitement? I want to introduce you to some of the top cookers who you may not know, after we beat your ass in this contest, of course."

Chapter 31

And they did. Once again, the women beat the men in the barbeque Battle of the Sexes. The men blamed that damn crown, but everyone knew it was because of their leadership void. It would take a long time for the Male Chauvinist Pigs to find someone as uniquely qualified as Pigpen Hopkins had been, someone who really put his heart and soul in the job, although Cork Stuecheck seemed to be having a ball in his roll as stand-in. He had real potential as a sideshow barker; he talked people into voting with pithy comments about their clothing or hair color. "Everyone who wore shorts down here on an October day has to vote twice," or, "Bald heads, over here," were his typical comments. For someone who had acted like a recluse a few days before, Cork was amazingly social.

"Heaven, are you ready, babe?" It was Murray Steinblatz calling out to Heaven from a golf cart. Murray had also been assigned to the booth-decoration judging team this week. The booth judging was to take place from two-thirty to three-thirty, about the time a team's last meat entry was due at the judging tent. Teams usually had one person assigned to the on-site booth decoration when that was part of the voting process. It made for a frantic day for the teams, but by three-thirty they could start breaking down their areas. The scoring results would be announced at four-thirty. Heaven jumped on the cart, waved at her teammates, who were getting quite rowdy celebrating in their tiaras and sashes, took her own tiara off and grabbed a decor ballot.

The first really decked-out campsite Murray and Heaven found was number twenty, a cooking team from just outside Topeka, Kansas. This was Heaven's home territory. Having grown up in the Flint Hills west of Topeka and east of Abilene, Heaven knew there were plenty of good ranch cookers in those rolling hills. She also knew the natural disposition of a Kansas rancher would be averse to running around the country cooking hunks of the meat he or she helped raise for prize money. So she was glad to see these two young couples who had decorated their booth with a *Wizard of Oz* theme. A yellow brick road was painted on the ground, and everyone on the team was in costume as the Cowardly Lion, the Tin Man, Dorothy or Glenda, the Good Witch. They even had a small dog named Toto. Part of the decor judging was actually being served some product. This booth was offering some spicy chicken wings, as well as brisket. Heaven took a small bite of the chicken, which was smoky and tender, and then marked her ballot. She gave them a ten, the highest score possible. By using grade-school visuals—that is, by looking sideways at Murray's ballot—she could see he gave them a ten as well.

"It'll be hard to top this, babe," Murray muttered under his breath.

"Murray, remember we're not supposed to judge them against each other. If we think they all deserve tens, that's what we give them, just like when you judge the meat entries inside."

"Yeah, yeah, yeah. You know what I mean." Heaven and Murray passed another cart full of judges.

"How many teams of judges are there, Murray?" Heaven asked.

"Six teams of two, babe. Everyone from swishy interior decorators to the artistic director of the Coterie Theater. And us, of course."

"We, who are the experts on visual good taste. Oh, Murray stop at this one." Murray and Heaven had been trolling past three or four booths, stopping and starting, jumping off to get a better view of some prop, then going on to the next campsite. Now they were in front of a giant teapot. It was made of burnished aluminum or stainless steel and smoke was pouring out of the spout. As Heaven and Murray came up to the booth, the team members opened the side of the teapot. Inside it was a huge smoker, with rotating round racks. The teapot team offered the judges some delicious country sausage from inside. As Heaven jumped back on the cart, Murray was marking his ballot in amazement. "Boy, these corporate sponsors will spend the dough, won't they, H?" A major tea company had their logo painted on the side of the teapot smoker.

"Well, Murray, barbeque is big in the South. Most of the tea sold in the United States is sold as iced tea and iced tea is also big in the South. I guess it's worth it to them to woo the barbeque fans."

"Yeah, well, what's their excuse?" Murray asked as they passed a booth sponsored by a Missouri banking chain.

"Barbeque fans have money now. It isn't just a poor people thing. Look at all the BMWs in the parking lot."

"Well, I know you have to be rich or have a rich sponsor to be a competitor, that's for sure," Murray said as they passed the motor homes and trailers and flatbeds and elaborate tents and wagons that transported this gypsy band from one contest to another.

American flags, Confederate flags, the flags of Kansas, Missouri, Georgia, Mississippi and South Carolina were all in view as Murray and Heaven continued their tour. Homemade banners with team names, pigs, and other livestock flew from the top of flagpoles.

One team smoked their meat in an old airplane fuselage and wore vintage bomber jackets and white scarves around their necks. One team had a giant pink pig for their smoker. Aza had a shack that resembled the rib shacks of the Old South. Felicity had a plantation theme, all lace and silver serving pieces. There were fake colonial columns at the entrance to her area.

Then there was Bo. The chuck-wagon, the cooking pit and the vintage cowboy attire were even better in daylight than they had been when Heaven and Bo had spent the evening together on Thursday. The chuck-wagon guy, Buzzard, was there telling tales of Texas roundups and dynamiting for water wells. There was a crowd of kids gathered around listening to his every word.

"The oral tradition isn't completely dead, Murray. This is good stuff to tell kids about."

"Kids, hell. I came over and listened to him for an hour last week. I'd love to do a story . . ."

"Murray, do you realize what you just said? You said you'd like to do a story about something! That is the first time I've heard you say that, you old diehard. The journalist in you rears its ugly head once again."

"Yeah, well, so I said it. I haven't written a letter in years, let alone a story. I probably couldn't write if I wanted to. You can't not practice the violin and then expect to be able to play Handel."

Heaven shook her head as they cruised to their next stop.

"The difference is, you still use language every day, even if you're not writing, Murray. If you're not practicing the violin, you're not using those skills. You'll be just fine, you'll see."

"But who would I write for?"

"Don't tell me you don't think a story about the World Series of Barbeque would be of interest anywhere. How about calling up your old boss, the *New York Times*. Can't you see this in the Sunday magazine?"

"You know they don't take stories written on spec, Heaven." Murray was talking negatively, but his face sure looked positive. He had a gleam in his eye that Heaven hadn't seen since spring, when Murray had done some sleuthing to help the cafe out of a jam.

"Well, then, what about proposing a column about things

here in the Midwest. One week it could be about barbeque, the next about a gang murder, the next about a quilt show. Whatever catches your eye and interest. You could call it 'Letters from the Interior.' That sounds exotic enough to get the attention of *Times* readers.''

''Sounds to me like you've got this all figured out. Maybe I'm not ready yet, H. I just don't know.'' Murray looked like he knew but was scared by his desire to write again. Sometimes Heaven thought that Murray believed it would be wrong to be fulfilled; to do meaningful work again. Since his wife couldn't come back to life, he shouldn't have a life either. His writing had won Murray two Pulitzer Prizes. Not writing was his way of being faithful to Eva's memory.

Heaven gave him a kiss on the shoulder. They were back at the judges' station. ''Well, just think about it, Murray. You've still got some stories in you that are dying to get out.''

There was an hour until the results of today's round of cooking were announced. Then someone would have a check for fifty thousand dollars for first place. Second place was twenty-five thousand, a big step down in prize money. Third was ten, fourth was five. That left ten thousand dollars for miscellaneous awards, such as best sauce and best booth decor.

Heaven wanted to go to the chili cook-off but she knew she should check the Que Queens' campsite first. She would then hunt down Bonnie Weber to tell her about Cork, and how strange it was for him to show up at a cook-off, how familiar his car looked. Heaven had been beating herself up for not spotting his car when she went out to his place but she didn't recall seeing any cars at all. They must have been in a garage.

When Heaven arrived at the Queens' home camp, there was a salon going on, conducted by none other than Dwight Brooks. He was signing autographs and a loose guitar told Heaven that he had been singing. Women of all shapes and sizes were crowded around. Dwight saw Heaven and grabbed her hand. "Heaven, honey, I've been havin' the time of my life with your girlfriends. How did your judging go?"

"Look around. Everyone went all out for the booth decoration this year. It was spectacular."

"Too bad you couldn't enter with this crown," Dwight said. "I had a hell of a week, Heaven, a hell of a week."

"Yeah, me too," Heaven said dryly. "What did you do from Monday until last night? By the way, thank you again for Monday, you made fans out of diehard hipsters."

"I love a tough room, Heaven. I do some of my best work in tough rooms. And this week, I traveled all around the area, tasting barbeque, visiting with folks. My vice president in charge of research and development flew out to join me. We went down to Wichita and up to Omaha, eating our way, of course. Then we went down to the Branson area, in southern Missouri. I play down there every year and I'd eaten some good lamb at a place out of town a-ways. Yes, Heaven, we had a car and a driver and we'd pull up to these places, you know the ones where the smoker on the outside is bigger than the actual cafe. They got a real kick out of it, this country music fella pulling up in a limo and orderin' one of everything."

Heaven thought of Murray. The image of Dwight Brooks and some fast-food executive cruising the three-state area in a limo that must have smelled like a smokehouse was priceless. If this didn't make Murray want to write "Letters from the Interior," nothing would. She patted Dwight and asked him to wait and go over to the announcements with the Queens. He said he had plenty of babies to kiss and turned back to his audience. Dwight knew his people. He probably could take something as unique as barbeque and mass market it perfectly. Heaven hated him for it, but with grudging admiration.

She spent the next few minutes figuring out what had happened since she and Murray had been gone on their judging tour. The answer seemed to be very little. Nothing had been put away.

The victorious women's team had popped some sparkling wine to celebrate, a Spanish cava, Segura Viudas. They'd even invited the men's team to celebrate with them in a move toward rapprochement that Heaven did not entirely approve of. Cork was there, lounging in a lawn chair looking like he didn't have a thing on his mind. Heaven looked around for Bonnie. She had expected to see the detective somewhere on her tour of the grounds, but she hadn't. She knew that Bonnie would be at the grand finale in a few minutes. Heaven looked at Cork, then she looked at Dwight. What characters this sport attracts. Not that she and the Que Queens were boring little cookie-cutter wives.

Heaven carefully studied all the people milling around. I know half of the people in this little quarter-block area, Heaven thought. Of the ones I know or at least am on a first-name basis with, I could imagine most of them trying to scare me with a propane detector if they thought I wouldn't be hurt. I could even see a few of them beaning Pigpen over the head and ditching him in the sauce. They would be sorry afterward, but they probably wouldn't turn themselves in; they would play the odds that they hadn't made a mistake. If they were eventually caught, they would explain how Pigpen had made them so mad, how it had been an accident. I can even see someone poisoning Simone. I just can't see someone in this crowd chasing me down the highway and shooting a gun at me, especially Cork. It's so, so common.

"Come on, let's go up and see who gets the big check," Stephanie said with a slight slur in her speech. Stephanie could be classified as bedraggled. Her usual bandbox grooming had been eroded by having her sleep interrupted every two hours, by the fact that someone had tried to kill them or at least slow them down, by the fact that they had had a party last night and they were having one now. Luckily Stephanie's husband, the lawyer, had come down when Sally Jo had called him earlier. For a change, he didn't act like the total uptight creep that Heaven usually thought he was. He must have understood that Heaven and Stephanie were mighty shaky today.

As the time for the awards presentation grew closer, the teams wandered up to the stage area, dragging their folding chairs and beer coolers with them. Everyone moved slowly after a night and a day of camping and cooking and drinking beer. The contest officials were rarely on time with the results. But this being the World Series, the committee was trying to be on schedule. Heaven and her crew were near the stage so when the committee members started gathering, they moved over where they would be able to see the next champion of the barbeque world be crowned.

Chapter 32

As the committee started its spiel, thanking the city and the sponsors and each other, Heaven looked around for Bonnie Weber. She spotted the tall blonde across the field. Also in view were all the principals of this little soap opera. Bo and Felicity and Aza were standing off to the side, apart from their team members. Cork Stuecheck was still in the Que Queens' group. Dwight Brooks had met up with his flunkies and was pointing out potential sauce donors.

Heaven checked her watch. She hoped the cafe was okay. About noon she had called in, not mentioning what had happened during the night. The restaurant wasn't open for lunch on Saturdays so the day crew came in late and the night crew came in early so they could knock out the prep work together. The place was fine at noon. Heaven knew that in the restaurant business a few minutes could change everything, let alone a few hours. She would call after the prizes were given out.

Heaven was happy to hear that her favorite couples from Kansas won the booth-decoration award for their Oz rendition. She was sure they could use the money. There had been three little children in their two families. Now it was time for the top four prizes to be given out. To say there was tension in the air would have been pushing it, but everyone had certainly quieted down, the high-fiving and the good-old-boy stuff had been retired temporarily. Fourth place went to the salmon smokers from Seattle. Heaven was worried about her new friends. If Ben Franklin had held on to first place then either Bo or Felicity or Aza had dropped out of the money.

Now everything went fast. Third prize, Felicity June Morgan, Charleston, South Carolina. Second prize, Eleazar Martin, Memphis, Tennessee. First place and the winner of the Second Annual World Series of Barbeque, wait, it's a tie, folks, between Ben Franklin, Kansas City, Missouri and Bo Morales, Amarillo, Texas. Everyone knows what that means, don't they, folks? Yes, according to the World Series regulations, tomorrow we will have a head-to-head contest. One meat: ribs.

It was the sudden-death playoffs of the barbeque circuit. Bo and Ben, in a photographer's wet dream, cooking ribs in the chuck wagon and the wok tower. Winner takes all the first-place prize money. The crowd went wild, whooping and clapping and starting to lay down bets.

The committee member called for attention again, announcing that tomorrow a new sauce contest would be held. It was added, he said, to give all the teams a reason to stay for the head-to-head but it also had the added prestige of being the first annual Smokin' Que prize. Dwight Brooks was paying the five thou in prize money and would every year from now on. The first-place sauce each year would be featured in his fast-food barbeque chain. Sounded like a cheap way to buy recipes, get advertising and also look like a nice guy, Heaven thought.

Heaven was heading across the area in front of the stage, looking for Bonnie Weber. She was intercepted by Felicity Morgan.

"We need to talk to you, sugar," Felicity hissed in Heaven's ear.

There was that "we" again. Maybe Heaven hadn't been as paranoid as she thought when Bo used that "we." Maybe it was a good "we."

"When and where?" Heaven asked. "And who?"

"You and me and Aza and Bo. Since Bo has to cook again, let's meet at his campsite in thirty minutes? I've got to go give my girls their instructions for breaking down." Felicity was toting a trophy the size of a Volkswagen. She waved the prize check under Heaven's nose with a grin.

"Yeah. I guess I have to go do that too. If I just had some girls to instruct," Heaven said as she looked back toward the campsite. Heaven hoped Barbara's boys were over there. She had no interest in breaking down that camp. And obviously by the way the camp looked when she got back from judging, no one else had any interest in breaking it down either. "I'll see you in a minute."

In the time Heaven had spent with Felicity, Bonnie Weber had disappeared. Heaven went back toward the campsite, hoping Bonnie would find her before she left. She discovered the elves from Barbara's staff, cleaning the smoker and drinking beer. Stephanie was being led away by her husband, Sally Jo had run off to the parking lot as soon as the tie was announced, Barbara had gone to her restaurant and Meridith was off to a wedding reception that she was catering. Heaven got her overnight bag and her knives out of the RV so the guys could move it when they were ready. Then she went to find a pay phone.

Cafe Heaven was busy, Murray said. They had a nice early crowd arriving now and two more full turns ahead. The kitchen seemed calm, Murray said. No one even asked about you. "Good, Murray. Hang in there. I'll be over to work the door with you later. But I'm not going to the kitchen to cook. I'll show them not to miss me," Heaven said and hung up the phone.

She headed across the rapidly changing village. The cookers had their camp breakdown figured out, like precision military grunt work. It looked like most of the teams were going to camp over another night, not wanting to miss the cook-off and sauce contest tomorrow. But they were packing up their supplies, loading their cookers on trailers and using their small grills to make dinner. Most teams brought a small Weber-style grill for times when the big smoker wasn't fired up.

The Bo Morales campsite was a beacon of warmth and light. Bo had lots of glass-shaded kerosene lanterns. They cast a spell of light and dark over the camp. The chuck wagon itself, with its web of skeletal wooden ribs, created a giant shadow, mythic and whale-like. The cooking pit still had wood embers glowing faintly. When Heaven arrived at the camp, Felicity was there and Aza wasn't.

Bo was toasting his team, most of them his family and neighbors. Heaven and Felicity stood quietly in the shadows. Bo raised his glass. "My family and some of your families have been in West Texas for generations. The Hispanic heritage·is part of the history of the West. Our families helped move cattle from the Rio Grande to Abilene and some of them undoubtedly cooked in chuck wagons just like this one. Because of all your help, we have brought the traditions of our grandfathers to the whole country. We are part of America's history and we have shown the country about their heritage, too. *Salud!*" Bo said solemnly and they all drank.

Heaven's eyes were filled with tears. This guy just killed her. She and Felicity gave each other the courtesy of not looking at each other and acting like old softies.

Soon the spell was broken. Bo started talking with his fireman about what woods to use on the fire tonight. Other team members went to feed the mules and pack up equipment they wouldn't need tonight or tomorrow.

"Aza, are you going to break down tonight?" Felicity asked as the big man appeared around the corner.

"I'm packing up the pickup with the shack and everything that goes with it. I asked the team what they wanted to do and most of them want to stay but two guys will drive the pickup back to Memphis starting tonight. The rest of us will stay for the grand finale. Can't leave our buddy without a cheering section, now can we?" Aza said, thumping Bo on the back.

Heaven wanted to be polite but she also needed to get to the restaurant. "What did you all want to see me about?"

Felicity took a pull on a long-neck Bud. "This is just between us, okay, Heaven?"

Heaven wasn't exactly comfortable with that. "Is this something that the police will want to know?"

Bo shook his head. "Probably not the police. Maybe the contest committee. We decided before we got here that we would pool our resources, one for all and all for one. I guess we were creating a barbeque version of the Three Musketeers."

"Wait a minute. What are you telling me? That if one of you had placed third, let's say, and the others hadn't placed at all, you would have split that money, what was it, ten thousand dollars, between the three of you? That you're going to split those checks you got today?"

"You've got it, sugar. It was a little insurance policy we took out, to make sure no one went home empty-handed. And also, we wanted to crush Pigpen. That was a big goal for us all," Felicity explained.

"As a black man, I've never had the time for revenge," Aza said, "but Pigpen called me a nigger to my face at Memphis in May. I've thought a lot about that since then. Yes, indeed. I wanted Pigpen to suffer."

Felicity threw a snapshot down on Bo's worktable. It was an old one of Paul Taylor and her behind a woodpile. Felicity was down on her knees and Paul wasn't. Bo threw another photo on the table. It showed him using an electric bean pot to cook his prizewinning cowboy beans. Aza looked grim and threw his photo down, one of him slipping already-cooked ribs in his smoker.

Heaven shook her head. "Pigpen was sure a sneaky guy."

"Hey, what can we say. None of us are proud of these things. They would never happen again," Bo said with pain in his tone of voice.

"These all arrived the week before we came to Kansas City, in a plain brown envelope," Aza said.

"There's more. Pigpen contacted all three of us after the photos showed up and offered to throw the contest for a price," Bo said with some degree of embarrassment. "We agreed to pay him a certain sum, uh, less than the amount of the top three prizes of course, but a nice sum anyway. Each one of us made a deal with Pigpen for the same thing, first place. He didn't know we were working together. We made a small down payment in each of our names. We told him we wouldn't pay up until after we had won. Pigpen understood that we couldn't trust him. Of course, we had no intention of paying up. We were looking forward to that moment when he realized he'd been stung."

Felicity added her two cents' worth. "Pigpen also bragged to me that he had a bidding war going on between a country star and a cookbook author for his sauce recipe. He said dealing with me and with them was more profitable than actually cooking. He said the cookbook author had told him she would double any offer the country singer made. Now we wonder if maybe Simone was just jacking with her ex-husband, making him spend more money than necessary out of spite. Now that we know he was her ex-husband."

Heaven saw possibilities here. "Do you think Dwight found out and killed Simone in a rage?"

Aza shook his head. "Who would have told him? Pigpen was long gone and Felicity didn't tell him. Surely Simone wouldn't mention it to Dwight, especially when the recipe had disappeared."

Heaven wagged her finger at Aza. "You are in the middle of a divorce. Can't you see Simone telling Dwight how she had driven the price up on him by ten thousand dollars just to see him steam?"

"Good point," Aza conceded

"Because there's more," Bo said. "We did want revenge as much as we wanted to win. So we bought some insurance. We paid someone to mess up Pigpen. We said mess up his sauce, break his smoker, sabotage his pickup. But we wanted him there, to be miserable. We never said anything about killing him, we just wanted to throw him off his game. We wanted to really make him suffer, not put him out of his misery.'' Bo couldn't help laughing and soon all four of them were enjoying the lost fantasy of seeing Pigpen out-maneuvered. They all confessed how they would have made him pay if they'd had the chance.

Heaven had laughed along with the rest of them but she had found Pigpen's body, so her perspective was slightly altered. ''So, what are you afraid of, that the person you hired accidentally killed Pigpen instead of just letting the air out of his tires?''

Felicity held up both hands. ''Just like anytime you en-trust your dirty work to someone else, Heaven, you run into trouble. We order one thing and the next thing we know, there's a dead body involved. Our guy is sure that the man he hired didn't do it. Then we hear this whole story about the missing sauce recipe. Where the fuck is the recipe? We sure don't have it. And now, today, our guy might be in danger. We're getting nervous. What if someone really had a hard-on for Pigpen and used our little scheme to kill him and is going to pin it on us somehow? What if this nut tries to take us out too?''

Heaven started pacing around the campfire. ''I can't really help you if I don't know who you hired. I probably can't help you anyway but I really can't help if I don't have the whole picture.''

''Hold your horses, Heaven. We agreed among the three of us to tell you what we know. It's just that we don't know everything. It was Paul Taylor we called to set up Pigpen. There's bad blood between them and it turns out that the sauce recipe is a big part of it. After Pigpen died it came out that Dwight Brooks had called up Pigpen and offered him big money for the sauce recipe and Pigpen wasn't going to share with his old partners.

''Pigpen and Paul and a third man all worked out that

sauce recipe and used it when they cooked together. They agreed to split the profits from making the sauce but only use Pigpen's name on the label.

"Paul told you this but said he didn't know about this double cross?" Heaven asked, rolling her eyes. "Oh, right. It makes more sense that he did know and when you called up and asked for someone to put salt in the sauce or sugar in the gas tank, it was the perfect chance for his revenge."

Aza shook his head. "Paul says not, that Dwight called him *after* the murder and mentioned the recipe in passing. He was calling him not because he knew Paul was Pigpen's ex-partner, but because he was the president of the guild. He wanted to talk to Pigpen's team or his wife or someone. He still thought he had a deal for the sauce recipe and mentioned it casually. That's when Paul came out to the commissary and you were there, Heaven. When he couldn't find it and no one else had it, he smelled a rat. You were his first suspect, of course. His second suspect was the third man in the old sauce deal. Paul Taylor is in the hospital and it's because of the third man. He also thinks this third man killed Pigpen in a rage. But here's the problem. He won't tell us who the third man is."

"Shades of Orson Welles," Heaven cracked. This was as baroque as she liked it to get. "Let me try to sum up what we know so far. Item: Pigpen murdered. Third man. Item: I get shot at. Could be third man, could be Paul Taylor. Item: I get gassed in my RV. Must be third man 'cause Paul wasn't around. Item: Simone Springer dies of anaphylaxis." Heaven looked around the group expectantly.

Felicity shrugged. "We don't have a clue, sugar. The only thing the two victims have in common is that Dwight Brooks was married to one and doing business with the other."

"I much prefer that link to the one Bonnie Weber came up with: me," Heaven said. "By the way, I still don't know what you want from me."

"We all might be in danger. You've been put in harm's

way twice. It didn't seem fair for you to not know as much as we know," Bo said with that corny tenderness oozing from every pore.

"Of course, if you told your big cop friend, we would deny all of it. We still are going to pool our winnings and we still would chip in to derail Pigpen, if someone hadn't done a permanent job of it. Paul Taylor is faking chest pains to stay in the hospital, he's so scared."

"I get the picture. This information is just so I might have a chance of staying alive through the rest of the weekend," Heaven said as she got up from the hay bale she'd been planted on. "What about Ben Franklin? Could he have anything to do with this?"

Aza looked over at Heaven. "We thought he could be the third man."

"Yeah, I suppose he could. I have another candidate that I might nominate, but not tonight. Tonight I have to go to the restaurant. Bo, be careful. If Ben is the third man, he might not play fair. Check your ribs, honey. I'll bring bagels in the morning." Heaven hugged all three of these conspirators.

She wanted to strangle them but she didn't have time.

Chapter 33

Heaven jumped in her van and cursed the marketing person who first thought of putting leaflets on cars. There were three stuck under her windshield after a day and a half at Barbecue Village. One, neon yellow, advertised a barbeque contest in Weston, Missouri, in two weeks. One, bright green, touted the sale of smokers at once-in-a-lifetime low prices. The third was plain white, folded over and taped shut with Heaven's name printed on it. Heaven threw the first two down on the floor of the van with the mail and tore open the one addressed to her. I THINK I KNOW WHERE THE RECIPE IS. MEET ME AT YOUR HOUSE AT NINE. PAUL. Heaven turned this piece of paper every which way, then dropped it on the floor with the rest. What do I expect, fingerprints, a Crain stationery watermark, engraving? Why my house? And I thought Paul was in the hospital. How did he manage to put a note on my car? I guess he could have had his wife or someone slip this note on here. Why is he being so secretive?

As Heaven backed the van out and headed for Fifth Street, she stopped and waved at the guard in the parking lot. At least someone will be able to say they last saw me on Saturday night, about eight, she thought. Quickly Heaven made her way to Columbus Park and opened the garage, hoping that by some miracle Hank's car would be there. She knew he was working till midnight but plans could always change. The garage was empty. Heaven had time to go in and pace for a while. She tried calling Bonnie Weber and Stephanie but no one was home. Because she was so antsy, she hung up both times before a machine asked for a message. Next she dialed the restaurant but the line was busy.

"Maybe I should write Hank a note, just in case this doesn't go well," Heaven said out loud. She went over to the kitchen desk and grabbed a piece of paper. She wrote: HONEY, I'M MEETING PAUL TAYLOR HERE AT NINE. DON'T. KNOW WHAT ABOUT. IF I'M NOT AT CAFE OR HERE, FIND ME. She folded it over and wrote HANK on the top, putting it on the big table that dominated the room. At eight forty-five, fifteen minutes early, the doorbell rang. "Thank goodness he's early. I can't stand another fucking minute," Heaven cursed as she ran to the door. The second the locks were released, the door opened and sure enough, there was Paul Taylor, complete with plastic hospital armband. But he wasn't alone. He was being followed by none other than Cork Stuecheck. Cork was holding the same big gun that Heaven remembered from the drive-by and he was pointing it at her again. This time his face wasn't in the shadows.

"So you put that note on my car, eh, Cork? I wondered how the patient here had managed that. Please by all means, come on in. I was on the phone with the restaurant. I'll be right back."

Cork reached out swiftly for Heaven's arm. "Nice try there. I see the phone and it's on the hook. What we need to do next is go find the jacket you were wearing Friday, Heaven. And remember, Paul will know if you're not telling the truth. Let's go upstairs."

Paul Taylor was not as smooth a bad guy as Cork. He avoided Heaven's gaze and seemed embarrassed. Heaven tried to use that. As they went up to the bedroom, she stopped on the stairs and turned to Paul abruptly. "Paul, whatever the deal is, why can't we talk it out, find a solution?"

Paul Taylor hit Heaven as hard as she had ever been hit

with the back of his hand. She saw stars and staggered. "Don't jack with me, Heaven. Everybody thinks they can jack with me. Get up the stairs and find that black leather coat."

Heaven felt Cork and his gun bearing down on her backside. She decided to not try the rational approach again soon. She burst into tears instead. Cork dug his nails in her arm and half carried her the rest of the way to the bedroom. "Nice try, Heaven. Save the tears, you'll need them later."

Heaven reached in her closet and pulled out the black leather jacket. "Later when I plead for mercy, eh, Cork? Did Pigpen plead?"

Cork laughed. "I'm not in a confessing mood, Heaven. I'm more in a cooking mood." He reached in the pocket of the jacket and pulled out a rumpled piece of torn paper. He straightened up and grinned. "And I needed a grocery list before I could start cooking. A grocery list that old Paul here ripped in two when he was interrupted in his final farewell to Pigpen, our old partner."

Heaven peeked at the piece of paper. She saw honey and beer and the names of seasonings. This must have been Pigpen's last shopping list, almost as good as the recipe. These guys could probably figure out quantities with the list of ingredients, at least after a few tries. Damn. Why hadn't she felt that piece of paper? She had been so focused on Paul that she hadn't seen him make the pass off. That's why they call it sleight of hand, folks. Of course, Paul wasn't exactly David Copperfield. This was probably more of an accident than a skillful plan. But it had fooled her.

Cork started unloading some supplies from his pockets, electrical tape and twine. Heaven had a feeling they were meant for her. She gave it one last try. "Look, Hank will be home any minute. You have what you want, I have no evidence about any of my wild speculations. Can't we just be friends?"

This time Cork pushed the gun into her stomach. "You better hope your boyfriend doesn't come home right now.

That would be very unfortunate for him. Paul, would you make sure Heaven doesn't scream? I'll drive with her and you can pick up the missing part of the list, since you have insisted on keeping it hidden.''

Heaven prepared herself for the electrical tape. Instead, Paul Taylor grabbed the gun and turned it around in his hand butt side out. He calmly knocked Heaven over the head with it and she fell like a sack of potatoes. Cork smiled, ''Big tough guy,'' he cracked and slipped the gun out of Paul's hand. He stuck it, along with the twine and tape, back in his pockets.

''I'm too old for this,'' Paul huffed as they hauled Heaven downstairs and into her own van. As they turned to leave, Cork spotted the note on the kitchen table. He picked it up quickly and read it. ''Good thinking, Heaven,'' he murmured and replaced the note where he had found it. While Paul took off to retrieve the missing half of the recipe, Cork drove Heaven's van, heading for the farm in Olathe.

Soon Heaven began to feel the stirrings of her senses that led her to believe that she was alive. She didn't really trust her senses, however, because the pain in her head was so overwhelming she couldn't feel the rest of her body. Maybe if I just close my eyes again, I'll wake up with my arms and legs. In a few minutes she took a peek through one opened eye. She was lying in the backseat of her own van. Cork was driving but she didn't even consider opening the side door and making an escape. Jumping out of a car going sixty down the interstate may have appeal on a day when you haven't already been slapped silly and knocked unconscious. Heaven played possum instead. Soon Cork pulled into the long driveway to his house. He jumped out and came around to open the side door for Heaven.

''Don't try anything silly, Heaven. I have nothing against you but you have definitely become a liability. Just come in the house with me and see who else is at our little party,'' Cork said cheerfully as he pulled Heaven toward the door with one hand on her legs and one on the gun.

Heaven didn't try the old boot-in-the-face trick. She got out as instructed and headed for the back door of Cork's house. As they entered the kitchen, she saw the other "guest" tied to a chair near the fireplace. She was a sight, bound in several different colors of electrical tape. It was Simone Springer, back from the dead.

Heaven marched right in and started yelling at her. "Thanks a lot for making me think I'd killed you with my peanut sauce. Thanks for not letting us know you survived. Murray was a mess. We all were. What about Detective Weber? And *what* are you doing here?"

Cork smiled. "Yes, isn't it a surprise now? Maybe I should let the lady tell you herself. Or at least her part of it." Cork pulled the tape off Simone's mouth. "Well, Simone, how did you get in such a fix?"

Simone was decidedly friendlier than she had been last week. She seemed positively thrilled to see Heaven and spill her guts. "Heaven, Murray and Detective Weber know I'm alive. Murray was real upset about not telling you the truth but when they gave me epinephrine at the hospital and I revived, Murray and the doctor called Detective Weber and she came up with this plan to just let everyone think I was dead and go ahead and investigate it as a homicide. After all, that was the intention, right? To kill me. Bonnie had me stashed at the hospital, thinking when the contest was over, if she still didn't have an arrest, I could just quietly get on a plane to Paris. Then I could announce my miracle recovery. It would have worked, too, except for the damn contest going into overtime today and Paul getting sick last night. I got so bored in my room, so I was cruising the halls last night and went down to the vending machines by the emergency room entrance. I spotted Paul when he and his wife came in and I tried to duck behind the Coke machine but I guess he saw me because early this morning, this maniac here came into my room and drugged me and put a coat around me and the next thing I knew, this." Simone gasped for breath after that. Heaven didn't let her catch it.

"Didn't you have a guard? What kind of a cockamamie scheme was this? How dare Bonnie and Murray not tell me. I can hardly wait to get my hands on them," Heaven snarled.

"I didn't have a guard because it wasn't known that I was alive. You have guards when there are big headlines in the paper that so-and-so is in such-and-so hospital after an attempt on their life. We wanted people to think the attempt on my life had been successful. Bonnie and her nice partner Harry Stein would come by a couple of times a day and bring me magazines and food and stuff. They said the hospital was safer than a hotel."

Cork was busy making a fire in the fireplace. He looked up and smiled. "So fate steps in. Isn't it wonderful? Paul Taylor has practically given himself a heart attack with worry and he goes to the emergency room and sees our little adventurer here. He calls me in a panic and I come save his sorry ass again. It was just like the old days."

Heaven started backing toward the kitchen thinking Cork was occupied, but before she got very far, he grabbed her ankle and pulled her feet out from under her. "Do you like to make fires, Heaven? Just be good now and help me make us a nice fire." Heaven crumpled some newpaper and stuck it in the cracks between logs. Cork continued chatting cheerfully.

"I had hoped to pin Simone's death on Dwight Brooks, especially when everyone found out what a dirty trick she was trying to play on him, making him pay double for the best sauce recipes. What a nasty little trick, Simone."

Just as Heaven opened her mouth to ask who actually put the peanut sauce on Simone's plate, her prime suspect for the job walked in the back door.

"Oh, good. You're back," Cork said to Paul Taylor. "Help me tie Heaven to this chair. I need your help loading that wood in the car. I want to deliver it while it's still dark."

Paul sat Heaven down in another dining room style chair

and went to work with the rope and then the tape. Heaven kept asking questions. She had a feeling her talking privileges would be revoked soon. "What was the purpose of killing Simone, Paul? If you'd been successful that is."

"There was no purpose, Heaven. I was just supposed to do something to throw the scare into the whole lot of 'em. I'd been thinking about leaving the party and going down to the parking lot and setting a fire. Then I heard Simone talking about how she was allergic to peanuts and there was a sign on a bowl saying peanut sauce so I slipped some in with the Arthur Bryant's. That stuff is hot enough to hide anything." Paul looked up with something like pride.

"Now that's thinking on your feet, Paul," Heaven quipped as the black electrical tape flattened her ample bosom. "Ouch."

"Come out when you get Heaven secure," Cork said as he put on his jacket and work gloves. "This won't take long with two of us," he said as he went out the back.

"One more question, Paul. I can't figure this out at all. Why did you change the scores to make Ben Franklin the top scorer?" Heaven asked.

Paul gave Simone a couple of new rounds of tape but he didn't tape either of their mouths. He was going to let them talk themselves silly while they could. He turned to Heaven. "Pigpen made a deal with Ben Franklin. He turned his head on the re-do of the courthouse and Pigpen made him a barbeque champ."

"You mean you made him a barbeque champ. What did Pigpen have on you, that you would be so eager to help, even after he was dead?"

"Pigpen was a good photographer. He had some photos in an envelope at his lawyer's. If the lawyer didn't get a check, my wife got the photos," Paul mumbled as he went out the door. Heaven knew that from the lovely shots she'd seen earlier. She didn't want to imagine what Pigpen had caught Paul doing—probably something involving Felicity.

Heaven tried to bring Simone up to date but there was a

lot to tell. She was just on Thursday when the guys came back in the house.

"Sorry, ladies, you're going to have to be gagged now. We have a delivery to make," Cork said. He used dish towels and more tape. Now Heaven felt really helpless. She wasn't ready for Cork and Paul to tilt her chair and start lugging her outside like she was a hall table. They scooted her over to her own van and threw her in on the floor. In a minute they were back with Simone.

"Jump in, Paul. Let's stick these charming ladies in the tractor shed, where no one will see Heaven's van." Cork and Paul drove the van into an outbuilding big enough for a tractor and a couple of cars. Cork's Blazer was there and the back of his car seemed to be full of wood. Heaven squinted to see better from the floor. "I'm glad to see you have plenty of gas, Heaven. I think I'll turn on the heat for you. We wouldn't want you to get cold, now would we?"

Heaven looked desperately over at Simone. Being tied up in a van with the motor on in an enclosed building. Sounds like Cork is planning the big sleep. Simone was making whimpering noises. Cork looked back at her. "Good thinking, Simone. Paul, Simone wants to know if you brought your half of Pigpen's grocery list. I guess she still wants to outbid that ex-husband of hers, eh, Simone?" Cork said with a wink at the wriggling figure next to Heaven.

"Sure, I got it." Paul Taylor pulled the other half of the list out of his pocket. "I was thinking I could stay here and mix up a batch, so we would have it for tomorrow. Like you said."

Cork smiled at his friend in the passenger seat. "Stay here? Good idea." He quickly lifted his gun out from under his coat and shot Paul Taylor somewhere around the heart. The shot was deafening in the van. Heaven steeled herself for the next one, the one she was sure would be coming her way. Cork calmly took the half of the grocery list they had found in Heaven's coat and put it next to the half Paul had produced. "Murder and suicide, all for a silly recipe. Isn't it a shame," he said over his shoulder to Heaven and Simone. He was wiping the gun and placing it in Paul's limp hand. "Paul here probably felt guilty for killing his old buddy Pigpen, don't you think? Of course, he didn't really do that, but that's our little secret, isn't it, ladies?" With that he turned on the car, got out and went to his own. Heaven could hear its engine start and the shed door open and close.

They were alone, two chefs trussed like Christmas geese and one dead man.

Chapter 34

Bonnie Weber hung up the phone. Hank had apologized profusely for bothering her at home. He had worked until midnight at the hospital and it was almost one when he got to Fifth Street. Heaven's van wasn't there and she wasn't inside. The bed hadn't been slept in. Hank had called Murray. He thought he might have got it wrong, that Heaven was staying two nights down at the barbeque contest. Murray said he had expected Heaven to come to the restaurant but they had been busy. By the time he realized she never showed, it was late and he assumed she stayed with the cookers down at Kemper Arena. Hank paused, then admitted he had gone down there, to the barbeque contest area. A nice woman with a southern accent had given him a cup of coffee. Said she was expecting Heaven in the morning, that Heaven had promised to bring bagels. Hank said no one had seen Heaven since around eight the night before. After what had happened the week before, Hank was worried sick. He went back home and this time saw the note. He had gone right upstairs the first time and hadn't noticed it. He called Bonnie Weber and read it to her.

Now Bonnie was worried sick too. She told Hank she'd be right down, not to touch anything. She checked with the desk at the station, just in case. No one had reported seeing a wrecked van or a red-headed corpse. The only homicide so far was a fifteen-year-old white male. Bonnie gave the desk sergeant a brief rundown on Heaven and Paul Taylor, with instructions to beep her if anything came up. Then she snuck back in the bedroom and dressed quickly without waking her husband. Bonnie scribbled her family a message and left it on the kitchen counter, pretending to herself she really had a plan.

Heaven tried moving around. She jiggled her way closer to Simone, who was making little moaning sounds through the towel and the tape. Her foot hit something in the dark right behind the driver's seat. She tried to feel it with her shoe but the leg of the chair was also in the way. Suddenly the chair leg seemed snagged on something. Then Heaven knew. It was her knife bag. One of the handles must have caught on the chair leg. Now if she could just get it closer to her hands, or to Simone's hands, maybe, just maybe, they could get a knife out before they passed out. She made all the racket she could and banged into Simone as hard as she could. Simone was turned away from her but she got the idea to roll herself around. Her head was at the opposite end, that is, next to Heaven's feet and the knife bag. When Simone flopped over, she saw the bag and knew what it was. Thank goodness I'm not trapped with an accountant or we'd never make it, Heaven thought. Heaven tried putting her weight behind the legs of Simone's chair, rocking her toward the knife bag. Simone threw her head toward it and was able to get behind it. The bag came loose and slid between the two women, who were rocking and rolling and shaking. Heaven was almost frantic. She knew time was running out. She was glad the shed was a big one. It would take a while for it to reach a toxic level of carbon monoxide. Simone had been able to undo the snaps on the bag with the very tips of her fingernails sticking out. Now they were both slamming into it, trying to jiggle a knife loose. Heaven heard a metal ping and something rolled her way. It was her potato peeler, which was not as sharp as a knife but it would do if she could just get a hold of the handle. She and Simone had adjusted to the dark and she saw relief in Simone's eyes as she spotter the vegetable peeler. Heaven nodded her head and kept rolling toward the knife bag so Simone wouldn't give up. Finally another metal clank and Heaven saw her needle-nose pliers loose on the van floor. They're a handy tool to pull the pin bones out of salmon. Heaven floundered around till she could semikick them toward Simone's hands.

In a couple of minutes, they had both managed to gouge a hole in the tape around their hands. Heaven had cut her palm but she didn't mind a bit. As she scrambled to untie her hands she saw Simone twisting the tape around the needle nose. She tore at the tape around her legs. As much as she wanted to get the gag off, she knew she needed mobility more. Soon Heaven was free enough to scoot to the van door, still dragging the chair, She pulled the van door open and hopped out, and continued to hop to the shed door, untying the rope that held her and the chair together. She opened the shed door, then took the time to remove the tape and towel from her mouth. She couldn't help but let out a war whoop as she went back to the van and helped Simone get loose.

"We did it. We did it. We're alive." She actually hugged Simone as she pulled off her gag. Simone threw her arms around Heaven. "I always tell my students having your own tools is important. Now I know why."

Heaven jumped into the front of the car and turned off the ignition, trying not to look at Paul Taylor.

"Is it bad?" Simone asked, peeking over the seat.

"For Paul, it's as bad as it gets."

"I guess we should call the police," Simone said as she dragged herself out of the car and tried to stand up. "Can't we have a nap and a drink first? Paul won't mind."

Heaven shook her head. "Paul won't mind but the next victims might."

"I guess you have a theory about Cork?"

Heaven went over to the woodpile. There wasn't much

left. She spotted what she was looking for, grabbed a log and then threw it in the back of the van. "I think we can rule out something as rational as greed or a good scam as a motive for Cork. He obviously didn't want the recipe and the riches that were supposed to go with it. I think his goal is to ruin barbeque, to make it so no one will want to enter a contest ever again. He wants revenge and I think he has the ammunition in the back of his car."

"The wood?"

Heaven opened the door to the passenger side. "I know this is gross but I think we should just take Paul with us and drive like hell to get to the contest. It's already six. It'll be light soon. We can put him in the back."

Simone stomped her foot. "No way. Then I'd have to sit where he just—no way. I'll just get my chair and ride in the back." Heaven did have a back seat for the van but she usually left it out to be able to carry more food and stuff.

"OK, but we have to go in and get a sheet or something. I refuse to drive down the road with a bloody stiff right next to me, God rest his soul." Heaven ran in the house and came back out with a blanket. She gingerly draped it over the victim. He slumped forward.

Simone sighed and picked up some of the rope that had previously kept her captive. "I guess I'm going to have to tie this dead body onto something so he doesn't come loose and destroy evidence. Ugh," she said with a wrinkled face. Three or four loops around the blanket and she tied a slick nautical knot to the armrest. "That oughta keep him. Let's get out of here," Simone said as she climbed in the back and closed the side door.

"Nice knot tying. Where'd you learn?" Heaven asked as she backed out of the shed.

"A French naval officer," Simone said with a smile.

Chapter 35

It was a strange, almost supernatural daybreak at Barbeque Village. The smoke around Bo's wagon softened the edges of everything, reminding everyone of the Civil War, something romantic and tragic at the same time.

The smoke billowing out of Ben Franklin's towering wok inferno smacked of Rube Goldberg, or, at least, Monty Python. Every camera crew in the four-state area would descend on this scene in an hour or so.

Right now, the only thing descending was the Cafe Heaven posse, led by Detective Bonnie Weber. Behind her marched Murray, Hank, Chris and Joe. Jumpin' Jack was inspecting the perimeter.

Bonnie found Felicity and Aza at Bo's camp, drinking coffee and pacing. Bo was moving his ribs around in the embers of his pit. They all looked grim. "Can we talk about Heaven?" Bonnie asked.

Felicity looked up. "If we knew where to look, I'd go in a minute. When her boyfriend came down here last night I knew something terrible had happened. She said she had a candidate for the third man and then she took off. I bet she went to confront this goon and, and . . ."

Bonnie shook her head. "Not according to the note she left at home. She was waiting for Paul Taylor at her house. No one has seen them since."

"I thought Paul was in the hospital," Asa said.

"He checked himself out yesterday afternoon, along with Simone Springer."

"Simone?" everyone said, more or less at the same time.

"Needless to say it's a long story. The hospital revived Simone last Sunday. She still had a pulse, just barely, when we got her there. Lucky we were so close to the Med Center. I talked her into staying in hiding long enough to get this damn contest over with. I thought it would help me if the murderer felt successful. And I thought I could keep Simone safe in a hospital," Bonnie said with a catch in her voice. "I was a fool."

Felicity pointed her cup at the detective. "So now Paul Taylor has both Simone and Heaven and we don't know where?"

"That's about it," Murray quipped from the peanut gallery. "Bonnie has sent for a team to search all around here. We were hoping they'd . . ." Murray trailed off.

It was daylight now and the smell of bacon was in the air as remaining teams made breakfast. The first tourists were pulling into the parking lot eager to see the first head-to-head in Barbeque World Series history. The presence of a full complement of police officers peering in every nook and cranny only added to the excitement.

Ben Franklin and Mickey glared at the crowd around Bo's chuck wagon. "Hey, police, what's going on? Some cheap trick to stop Mickey and I from the prize? Well, no one's gonna stop us now, eh, Mick?" Ben grabbed two or three logs and stuck them in the woks that were the firebox. Hank walked over to the camp.

"Very ingenious use of woks," he said with true admiration.

"Well, these are from you people. I just added American know-how," Ben said.

"They certainly have your unique touch," Hank said sweetly. "Have you seen Heaven or Paul Taylor around?"

Ben shook his head. Mickey did the same. "I told her to

steer clear of me this weekend. I'll run her off if she steps one foot near my rig.''

''Why?'' Bonnie Weber asked sternly. ''Ben, this is an official investigation. If you know anything about Heaven you better let me know or I'll hold your little elf here over that pit of embers over there.''

Before Ben could come back with an equally crusty retort, the blaring of a horn made everyone turn their heads. Crashing through orange cones and campsites, a van appeared. It was heading straight for the wok tower and it looked like Heaven was behind the wheel. Beside her was a large form wrapped in a blanket, careening left and right as Heaven tried to dodge tent poles and trash cans. She came to a screeching halt right between the rival camps.

''Don't do it,'' Heaven shrieked as she jumped out. Simone Springer opened the side door and held up a log like it was a rattle snake. ''Don't use this kind of wood. It was put on your woodpile in the night and it's—'' Just then a gust of autumn wind caught the smoke curling out of the top of the wok and sent it toward the ground.

Mickey was the first to go. He crumpled like a Kleenex. Next down was Aza Martin, who caught a big gust of smoke as he ran across the camp toward Heaven. Heaven turned around just in time to see Ben Franklin land right on top of Bonnie Weber.

She grabbed Hank's hand and yelled, ''Everybody. Run downwind fast.'' About that time Murray got the brilliant idea to jump in the van. He opened the passenger door and out fell the body of Paul Taylor, the blanket coming undone.

As panic ensued and everyone left standing started yelling for help, Jumpin' Jack came running up with a fireman and a hanky over his face. ''Oleander. I recognize it from my tree-identification class in Scouts.'' The fireman had some sort of chemical foam and he doused Ben Franklin's fire, and his ribs. Jack started his unique first aid on the unconscious figures. ''Never roast your hot dog on an oleander branch,'' Jack proclaimed. ''Even the smoke can be deadly.''

Chapter 36

The room was crowded. Bonnie had walked down from her room to Aza's when she heard Heaven and Felicity brought food. Ben and Mickey were sharing a room nearby and Heaven had brought them a big plate of Felicity's spicy shrimp and grits.

They hadn't asked them to join in the champagne, however. Facing death together doesn't mean you have to be friends. And there were plenty of friends to celebrate with: Bo and Murray and Stephanie and the Cafe Heaven crew and Jumpin' Jack, the hero. His fast work had saved the day. The doctor wanted them to stay overnight for observation. Mickey was the hardest hit but even he was going to make it.

"I couldn't believe it when Cork Stuecheck walked calmly up with that shit-eating smile on his face," Felicity said as she popped another cork and filled Aza's paper cup. "Thank goodness Bo hadn't fed his fire since last night. That cookin' with embers saved our ass, honey."

"Yeah," Heaven agreed. "The poison guy said that if both fires had really been cranked up, hundreds of people would have been sent to the hospital. And that's exactly what Cork wanted. He wanted to spoil barbeque as a sport. If he couldn't have it the way he thought it should be, no one could enjoy it. He didn't try to escape though. I guess he needed to see the misery he caused more than he needed to get away."

"Revenge is a terrible thing. Simone's revenge almost got her killed. Cork's almost got us killed," Bo said as he slipped his arm around Heaven and gave a little squeeze. Heaven smiled and slipped out of Bo's arm. After all, Hank was on duty at this very hospital. No sense in tempting fate any more today.

Bonnie was sitting on the side of Aza's bed. She grabbed another helping of grits and shrimp. "So where will the next World Series of Barbeque be held? You guys aren't going to let a little murder and mayhem stop you now are you?"

"No way," Aza said. "Memphis will host the next championship and I intend to keep the big prize at home. By the way, what did the committee decide to do about the head-to-head?"

"Split the money between Bo and Ben and get everybody out of town while there's still some survivors," Heaven said. "Kansas City will never be the same."

Pigpen's Secret Sauce

2 cups apple cider
½ cup balsamic vinegar
10 oz. tomato ketchup
4 oz. each of honey mustard, yellow mustard, coarse-ground mustard, honey, molasses, and cane syrup
1 bottle dark beer
½ cup cold coffee
⅛ cup each of Worcestershire sauce, soy sauce, Louisiana hot sauce
1 tsp. each of ground black pepper, celery salt
1 habanero chili, diced, no seeds
pinch each of kosher salt, ground coriander

Combine all ingredients and simmer 25 minutes on low heat. Cool and refrigerate.

Bettina Bilby has agreed to board her neighbors' felines for a long holiday weekend: an expectant tabby, a pampered blue-eyed Balinese, a depressed ginger Persian with a cod-liver-oil addiction, and Adolf, an imperious mouser with a patchwork face.

But during a freak storm, a carrier pigeon is downed on the doorstep with a tiny load of large flawless diamonds. And Bettina's dilemma escalates as Adolf gobbles up one of the gems and a succession of elegant but shifty strangers prowl the gardens, offending the cats, and bringing in their wake back-door bloodshed and murder.

THE
DIAMOND
CAT

MARIAN BABSON